NOT A
GIRL

NOT A
GIRL

SHORT TALES...
...FOR DARK DAYS

CHRISTOPHER DONALDSON

Matador
9 Priory Business Park
Kibworth Beauchamp
Leicestershire LE8 0RX, UK
Tel: (+44) 116 279 2299
Email: books@troubador.co.uk
Web: www.troubador.co.uk/matador

ISBN 978 1784623 395

British Library Cataloguing in Publication Data.
A catalogue record for this book is available from the British Library.

Printed and bound in the UK by TJ International, Padstow, Cornwall
Typeset in Aldine by Troubador Publishing Ltd

Matador is an imprint of Troubador Publishing Ltd

Cover photography by John Seymour

CONTENTS

THE WAKE OF THE BANSHEE

My name is Conrad Lettinger and I am skipper of the *Banshee*. I am fifty two years old and the boat somewhat older, although she creaks less and wears her years better. She's a sloop out of New Victoria. She's my lady, the only one now, and right at this moment we are both where we belong. In my life, three women have said they loved me and two of them have meant it. None however, have loved me like this fine girl, and none have been abused as much.

I'm nestled in behind her wheel now, and its smooth oak tugs this way and that as our bow cuts the swell. It parts both moonlight and spray, and aft, our wake shines as it boils away to darkness and the last lights of the land. I'm as happy as I can be, with a good wind and the boat set just right, a tin cup of something hard on the dash and a failing cheroot glowing its last. The memories come unbidden, and for the first time in a month I don't deny them space. Each one brings a smile or a wince, and then I throw it into the wake.

To drift to the land, or not.

*****

I find myself thinking of Annie. Annie who laid me down in the dry grass of the prairie in the last days before the

1

missiles fell. She was a farm girl, the child of my folk's best friend from college. I was a sea boy, unfamiliar in a landscape without coast and the scent of brine. It was a holiday of sorts, and in hindsight an excuse to get me gone for a month or so while my folks tried to make plans for the coming war, and some sense of what would follow.

We'd done the deed, and to my credit I don't think she ever knew it was my first time. She'd asked about the sea and I'd laughed, waving at the wide prairie.

"It's kinda like this," I'd said, buttoning my shirt, "but it's wet and it don't forgive."

"Are you and your folks staying where you are if the war happens?" she'd asked.

I'd shrugged. "No place else to be, Annie."

A week later she'd told me she loved me. I took a plane home the next day.

★★★★★

The wind has freshened somewhat and there are whitecaps here and there, while the moon is off to port and has the sky to itself. I've got the beacon loud and clear, and the helm 'puter recommends 10 degrees to starboard. Naa, not yet. I'll reckon it later. I plan to approach them on a close tack, long and slow. Give 'em time. Give me time. I refill the mug and another memory is consigned to the sea.

★★★★★

2

It was a strange kind of war; confused, short and brutal. Both sides – or should I say all sides – had weapons we'd had no prior knowledge of. Yes there were missiles and destruction, but there was also a creeping death that seemed to take folk at random. Most went weeks after the strikes, but some lasted months – wheezing their last while what medical care remained struggled to even understand what ailed them.

The big difference was scale. Most wars take some and leave most. This bastard took most and left scant few of us. I laid my folks in the ground five weeks after the government, or what was left of it, gave up and went off the air. I was sixteen. Preacher McDonald read the words and most of the town came along; even then we'd started to take more care of our community, what was left of it. Our little town by the sea became our world. We farmed, grew crops, and in a way gave thanks there were so few of us. There was always just enough.

Don't get me wrong, we had commerce. There were towns up and down the coast and we moved as freely as we wished. It's strange, everyone's idea of a world after the apocalypse never came to be. No marauding gangs back then, no petty dictators rising up to fill the power vacuum. Not then. That may have been the case in the cities, but we were far out, and preferred it that way. No one tried to organise the world anymore, they just tried to organise their bit of it. In fact there were many who argued the quality of life was much improved. They were the older folk of course. Us young 'uns whined like young 'uns always do. Then we got old and a generation arose who

3

had no knowledge of the world before, and they just got on with it.

The Barbarys came years later.

Wind power and solar cells made most things go. Diesel and gas came infrequently, under armed guard from some enterprising guys in the old Navy yards up the coast. It was paid for with whatever we could. I kept a low stock myself, just enough for the days when the wind died and the sea became a silver mirror. Even then I'd be happy to drift a day or so until the heat and lack of food forced me to fire up the old John Deere Marine below decks.

I'd taken ownership of the *Banshee* when my dad passed, and sailed her most days, bringing fish and contributing what I could.

"Son," this was Eli Makepeace. "You can't sail that mother by yerself 'cept in the bay, and that when there's only two or a three blowing. She's a boat for a skipper and a hand, or maybe more."

I'd laughed in his face with the arrogance of youth. I'd crewed since I was four and I knew my boat. I could set things just right and, well I clipped on, right?

Sure I clipped on, and while that keeps you strung to the boat, it sure don't stop you falling over the side. I was heading home when it happened, some two miles out in a force five. We were on a reach with the bow dug deep and a good lean on. I tripped, slipped or whatever, and then I was breathing the cold sea, towed from the waist through my own wake. It had taken me half the way to shore, and more strength than I knew I had to pull myself back. Thank God I left the ladder down through habit.

I'd collapsed on the deck with bloody hands and my arms nearly out of their sockets.

I guess I lost most of my arrogance that day. The ocean is a tough teacher – she gives her exams first and her lessons afterwards...

Anyway, a couple of days later I'd regained a little of my damaged pride. Hogie, Tom and myself had ridden his dad's wagon up to Bedford, the next town north. We'd taken a crate of homemade hooch and some high hopes along for the ride. Bedford was about the same size as our small harbour town, but it was just a little wilder. Sure enough we hit straight in the middle of a street party. We'd wandered around a while as the violins played some energetic scratchy folk stuff from way back, and as the sun went down the people danced. I don't recall how it happened, but I found myself bumping up to a pretty blonde called Daisy. She had a wide smile and a dress that floated up high as she jiggled around. Maybe it was the hooch, but two hours later we lay on the veranda of her beach house, playing with each other's hair as the night wind dried our sweat.

I'd stayed a week and we hardly left the house. We'd lie in bed and pretend we heard aircraft, or the newscasts on TV. We'd dream of times past and make plans for Paris or Rome, not knowing if they were even still there. After six days she'd told me that she loved me. I'd given her a holding smile but didn't reciprocate. Next day we'd parted and I'd promised to return. I finally made it back in a borrowed buggy a couple of weeks later. I found her in the sack with a local guy. She'd given me a frank open smile and a long kiss. I'd wished them well and drunk myself

5

stupid on the ride home. Who was I to judge? We had to make of the world what we could, and she was a burning fire, hungry for happiness where she could find it.

★★★★★

That memory goes over the side too, and that's when I see their lights.

Two bright beams are sweeping the waves less than a mile off the starboard bow. I know these are the Sixer's searchlights, fore and aft. The Barbarys aren't concerned with marine etiquette or normal running lights. They want to be seen only on their terms, and they've undoubtedly tracked me for some time.

Well boys, here I am. Hope you brought beer.

I reel in the main sheet and bring the *Banshee* round some ten degrees. My jib flaps in protest, sure that she's been ignored. She gets tightened too. For some reason I turn around and look back along the fluorescence to the thin margin of darkness that is the last of the land. There's the odd bright speckle, and a faint irregular orange spark that has to be Marvin's beach fire. It's lit for me, and I suppose is some kind of metaphor for a hope of sorts.

We'll see.

★★★★★

The Barbarys had shown up a month ago. They had ridden in fast and loud on the morning tide, right down the line of the low sun. Their huge black diesel boat, a converted MTB from way back, belched smoke and probably burned more fuel than we thought was left in the world. It had no name on the bow, just three digits, 666, crudely painted and bright yellow.

They called it the Sixer, it brought with it dread, and the end of most of our peace of mind.

Someone with a twisted sense of history named them 'Barbarys' after the pirates of old. But these were no seafaring scoundrels, no sir. They were rapists, thieves and butchers.

Their leader was called Rake, a huge buffed Caucasian with a bald head and tattoos on his face. He strode ashore from one of their inflatables ahead of the pack. They were a mixed bunch of Negros, Asians and white men, armed to the teeth and dirty as hell.

They had no fear or doubt. None. Rake's calling card was an M16 that he fired into the air.

"What you folks got here? You got a leader? Get him here now."

Well, we'd kept the old system the best we could over the years. In the absence of an army we'd maintained what stood for a police force. They deputised and changed as the years passed. At that time old Tommy Jones, God bless him, had the title of sheriff. He wasn't equipped to deal with the drunken brawls that sometimes broke out on a Saturday, and he sure as hell couldn't deal with this. I'll give him his due though, he strode down the beach that morning, beer belly sucked right in, trailing Matt Pine his deputy, and looking for all the world as though he would send those men back where they'd come from.

At a range of ten yards, Rake shot them both to pieces. Then he lit a cigar as they bled out onto the fine sand.

It took a few seconds for the first scream, during which time the fading echoes of the discharge bounced around the buildings and hills. There was pandemonium for a short while. Then one of the men passed Rake a loud hailer.

"This is how it's gonna be, folks. I want someone who knows this town and its supplies down here right now. They might live if they tell me the truth. We want most of your grain and whatever meat you've got on ice. You will load it onto these dinghies. These men behind me are gonna make a little tour of this fine village you've got here. You will give them what they ask for, or they will take it and kill you."

He took a long breath.

"Now, maybe there's some among you, some young bucks with guns stashed at home and more balls than sense, thinks they can take us and end this. Well you can't. We are meaner and dirtier than anything you've got. We will kill you in a moment and then find anyone who was near and dear and they will suffer. I hope I'm clear."

I was crouched in the *Banshee*'s cockpit at the time, moored to the harbour wall, hunkered low. From where I was I counted eighteen men on the beach and at least ten more on the Sixer, all armed. Yep, he was clear all right.

An hour later and they had all they wanted stacked on the beach. They hauled old Angus Berry, the mayor, down to the shoreline. Rake invited everyone to gather there. Most did. I did.

"Now listen good. You folks still keep a calendar?"

Angus nodded meekly. Rake laughed out loud.

"Well good, so do we. That calendar is now your friend. The date is April 26th, am I right?"

A nod.

"Good. We will be back in exactly four weeks. May 26th, before the weather comes in bad. We'll take your diesel then. But just in case you're thinking to organise, we'll take it out at sea. You will bring a boat to these co-ordinates…"

He handed Angus some paper and scanned the seafront and harbour wall.

"Who owns that sloop?"

To their credit no one spoke. About ten pairs of eyes however, turned in my direction. I held his gaze and stuck out my chin. My chest felt tight.

"That thing got a hatch to the hold big enough for ten diesel drums?"

No point to lie.

"Uh huh. Forward of the mast."

He nodded.

"Alright then. That boat, those co-ordinates, that date. Midnight. We'll be showing spotlights when you get close. Am I clear?"

I looked up and down the beach. Two hundred pairs of silent eyes regarded me. From somewhere behind Rake came the click of a weapon being cocked.

"And then you'll leave us alone?"

He laughed. If you had heard it in any other context you would have thought him genial. It was an open honest laugh, like you might hear after a genuinely hilarious joke. The laugh of a man who loves the world and what it has just offered him. He turned to the scum that had followed him up the beach and invited their incredulity. Then he turned back to me.

"And then my friend, we'll do what the fuck we like. Y'see, we're new in these waters. We like your little folksy towns and their cute survivor mentality. I figure you ain't seen the reality of this new world of ours proper like. Well, we're your new reality, and your priority from now on is getting as few of you as possible killed."

He brought up the loud hailer again.

"There is one more thing you people of this little town should know. There are plenty more of us. If you get organised and armed, it will be a short fight. If you figure you can somehow defeat us with numbers then you're wrong. You may damage us, but I promise you will see horror like you can't imagine. You may find this hard to believe, but I'm the only thing holding these sons of bitches in check."

He motioned behind him.

"Yep. I'm the nice one. Think on that."

Someone close by cleared his throat, and I thought for a moment old Angus was about to make a speech. I was wrong. Rake leant on his gun and looked up and down the beach. His gaze stopped some twenty yards to my right.

A woman had stepped out from our ragged line. She wore a short summer dress that was bleached out and faded. It stuck to the front of her and washed around behind as the morning breeze played with it. I had hung that dress on our line the day before, and watched it dry in a similar breeze. She took a step back as he drew up to her, but her head was high and her eyes cold. I loved her for that, but I had lead in my stomach for what might happen next.

"What gives you the right, you bastard? What gives you the right to mess with us like this?"

Her hand was shaking and tears rode down her cheeks as she gestured to where old Tommy and Matt lay. Her voice rose and cracked.

"These…these men had families. This a peaceful place. This is… you dirty bastards."

Oh Jesus. Maggie, shut up girl.

Lizzie Ghent from the old post office grasped her wrist and tried to pull her back, but she shook free. Rake towered over her. His voice was surprisingly soft now, but it carried to me.

"I'm not gonna ask your name sweet pea. I'm gonna call you 'random girl'. It may have escaped your attention that there's been neither police force nor military these past thirty six years. 'World's kinda reorganised itself, see? Things pan out a lot simpler now. Sure some of you get along just fine, but the way we see it, there's right and there's might. We chose might because it was all we knew. So I guess the might gives us the right."

He nodded, evidently pleased with his logic.

"Maggie, back off girl. Back off now."

I heard the words come out, but felt no ownership, only dread.

"Now, Mr Boatman here seems to have some sense random girl. Why don't you…"

She slapped him quick and hard.

There is such a thing as a collective gasp, I heard one then. Rake took two steps back, and Maggie brought both hands up to her cheeks as he levelled his weapon. He fired a quick short burst into her midriff. It took her life and mine, and it took the soul of our little town by the sea.

★★★★★

That memory is heavy, and as I haul it over the stern, most of me wants to hang on. I want to hug it close as we slowly barrel down through the pitch water and cold. I want it to be the last thing with me as the pressure takes my air and pain, and the dead eyed fish come to feed.

Not yet.

The two searchlights are sweeping in front of my bow. They have the sense not to blind me at least. The *Banshee* is hauled up real close the wind, and the jib has started to luff. There are two hundred short yards to run. In spite of the moon, there's no reflection from the Sixer's matt hull, but she is bow on to me, and I can see her silhouette as though she's been cut from black card and stuck to the sky. I aim to bring my boat to a dead stop on her port beam. It has to be like that. I must make the delivery. We had a deal.

An amplified voice comes out of the dark.

"There you go, Mr Boatman, dead on time and in the right place. Guess there's still some sea skills in this sorry world. Looks like you're riding heavy as well – that better be with diesel."

I wonder at this man's history. Navy man? Marine gone wrong? Hell knows. He's right about the *Banshee* riding heavy… and there is at least some diesel.

★★★★★

Maggie and I had drifted together. There had been no explosion of lust or need – we were both a little old for that. She had been a neighbour, some six years my junior and tied to two elderly parents who had survived the war, but succumbed to a loss of faculty as the years rolled on. Thankfully they had passed within weeks of each other about five years ago. Maggie had no shortage of comfort from the town, some of it from me, and out of that something blossomed. She blossomed. I attributed her change to the lifting of responsibility, but she seemed to suddenly want to engage the world. She certainly engaged me, and the love that grew in a few short months was deep and abiding. I'd never known anything like it and I don't think she had. I think it was also a product of this new ragged world. Seize the day they say. We had.

Given that she had lived her life by the sea, before and after the war, she had never had much to do with boats. Anyone that gets close to me however has no choice. She had taken to sailing like nothing else. Most folks act predictably their first time out in a good wind. They try to counteract as the boat leans and make for the windward side, their logic can't cope with the fact that there are two tons of steel beneath the waterline and this thing just ain't going to roll over. There was none of that. She did what she was told, and did it with a young girl's eyes glowing in a woman's face.

The most significant thing I can say about us is that I forgot what life was like before her. I couldn't imagine a time when she wasn't around.

I still can't.

★★★★★

My wake is almost gone now as the *Banshee* slows. I decide to keep this memory with me. There are a number of men on deck, and the moon makes the barrels of their weapons shine. Ten yards out I give the wheel a flick to starboard and drain my cup. I drop it onto the deck and pick up the small switch box that Marvin has rigged so carefully. I follow the wire as it loops through the deck hatch, down through the cabin, and into the hold. Its single light is glowing green, and I cover it with my hand.

Rake is in silhouette, braced against his wheelhouse. There is a short grind as our hulls touch and the boats roll together. His men tie us off fore and aft, and he lays his gun down.

"Nicely done, Mr Boatman. Now let's see what you got."

What I've got is two hundred pounds of C4 explosive in the hold. It's wired to a bank of batteries that had better supply enough charge to end the world. There is a newly rigged steel bulkhead on the starboard side that will hopefully push most of the blast to port through my hull and send the Sixer to the hell it surely longs for.

I wish I could see his face instead of a blank silhouette.

"Her name…" I shout. "I want you to know her name."

He leans down towards me and his men stop what they are doing.

"Who's name, Mr Boatman?"

I spread my arms, keeping the switch covered and praying to whatever that Marvin has half the skill he reckons.

"Random girl, you pig. Her name was Maggie. Maggie Riley."

I swear I can feel him tense. As her name leaves my lips, the wind takes the words and they scatter with the spray. They are drops of hope in the moonlight.

"She said she loved me, and I loved her. Am I clear?"

There's an instant when I think they know what's about to happen, and then I squeeze the switch. God bless you Marvin.

★★★★★

My name is Conrad Lettinger, and if there is such a thing as a moment between life and death then this is it. The moment contains many smiles and many drained glasses. It holds the scent of the sea and the glint of fish scales as they wash over the side on a bright day. It holds a hunger for love and an ache for things lost. It condenses everything that man has done up to that moment. It

15

doesn't hold the big things, not the race for the moon nor the lost promise of a cure for cancer. It doesn't hold the fine words or the empty guarantee of peace just months before our quiet apocalypse. It holds a humble love between many separate men and women, and it holds in its brief stare a single sail on a night sea, casting small memories into its wake as it heads towards an unknown horizon.

NOT A GIRL

The girl's body lies face down in the ditch, a pale spider embracing the saturated grass. The thin brown dress has become transparent, and clings to contour and crease. It isn't clothing now, more like a smear of autumn leaves, soaked and traffic-stamped into the highway.

He stares down at his discovery, tight-lipped and motionless, not knowing how to feel about what he has stumbled upon. The rain continues to fall, and the late afternoon light has washed most of the colour from the day. He can't acknowledge the rain anymore, or feel irritation, or cold, or anything. Once he lets these things back, so much more will come.

There will be far too much.

She died badly, that much he can see. The downpour has washed her head wound into the surrounding grass and the collar of her dress. He wants to move towards her, to act in some way, to do something right. But he can't. Somehow movement would release the feelings that are stowed safe and locked in tight, so just a while longer. Be still.

There is a gust of wind at his back now, although the day has previously been still. The air becomes ice and carries a sound from behind. He doesn't register it as a voice, although it speaks in a sibilant whisper. It carries

17

longing and panic and confusion, and it seems to carry shades of grey and deep shadow as it rounds his back, holds him, and bids him turn.

"I'm so far, so far."

For a moment he believes he has turned around to face the source of the words, but then he understands that they come from another place entirely, and from all possible directions.

"I'm in the cold. Make someone come."

He does turn now, but doesn't feel his feet apply the movement. His gaze rises slowly and reluctantly upwards. The girl who is not a girl stands ten feet away, although she doesn't stand, or float. She is simply there, and not just there, but all around. She is made of water, air and a white smoke that blurs any outline or definition. Her form seems pulled from the trees and damp air, and is formed of confusion as much as anything else, because right now what she feels is what she is. Soon she will be profoundly sad – he can feel it before she can – but for now her eyes reflect the pleading in her voice, as they widen and melt.

"You must call someone. I'm so far away," she falters, "and I'm here. Tell them to find me, to help me."

For a moment the small voice fades and is replaced by many. It sounds to him like interference, as though she has found a wavelength, but a shared one. He tries to pull his attention back to his place, the real place, the place where the girl is simply dead and cold, but real, and not this thing. He turns to regard the trees, the beech and maple whose branches shed the rain, and close around the track to the clearing where he stands. She pulls him back, and her voice has risen. There is a fierce urgency in her tone, and an anger that takes him beyond dread.

"Me! That's me."

She points a stiff arm past him, but the fingers hang limp, uncertain of their role in the gesture. The words continue to come, strangled and enraged.

"You…made…me…be…like…that."

Her eyes are desolate, and switch from him to the body in the ditch.

"Make me come back from here. Make me come back."

He tries to form words himself, and finds difficulty in the mechanism. He too gestures with unfamiliar smoke hands, and his voice rides on a wave of cold air.

"You can't come back, and nor can I. You saw to that."

His eyes drift down to the mud and long grass that lies flattened at the feet of the ghost girl. His own body lies there, shot to hell and twisted, wearing clothes he has already forgotten.

"You did me first… You thought it best. Then you did yourself. Look at the gun in your little white hand."

He feels the interference now, pulling this way and that, greetings and threats from cold things that have been here for so long. The girl that is not a girl meets his eye again. The interference is taking her too, and a last pleading look holds both regret and dread. A face sits next to hers and forms a raptor grin. Then she is gone, lost to the rain and the trees. Lost to him.

ALL OF THEM

I stop by the side of the lake to catch my breath. I've been walking quickly to catch up, slipping through the dense twilight and damp air, while a bank of heavy cloud stacks against the northern horizon. I'm in an elevated state of mind – it's been several hours now since the event and I've wandered much since, away from the deserted houses and the quiet town, into the country park.

I'm excited and more than a little unnerved by this new world. They really have all gone. There are just the two of us.

I saw the girl a while ago from the other side of the lake, just a small frightened figure at the margin of the water, walking this way and that. She's been scared out of her head since that moment when the world changed forever. She was shocked to the core, of course she was, one moment another straight day at the bank, and then this. I ducked out immediately to avoid being seen and I've tailed her since at a discreet distance – wary of making contact too soon. I guess I'll see her again when I clear the trees.

For me, the memory changes and becomes stranger as the hours pass. All the ones at rest or walking around just faded away. They dissolved in seconds as though they'd become soluble, the final strands of their existence whipping away on some cosmic wind. Their clothes crumpled to the ground, forlorn empty fabric. The more active or mobile ones pose a deeper mystery. They somehow seem to have received some seconds warning, conscious or otherwise of their imminent disappearance. There is not the traffic chaos, the carnage, I anticipated. There is evidence of them stopping their cars, slowing their trains before winding themselves away. I'm not sure about the aircraft though – I've heard no impact noise and seen no smoke – and I don't know about the boats. There must have been some minor disasters already – river cruisers and sailboats casting their empty hulls against deserted shores. There will maybe be some bigger wrecks as soon as the cruise ships and tankers find land. That'll be something to see. Maybe I'll get a car and some binoculars and drive to the coast. Maybe I'll take the girl. Yes, I'll take the girl. That'll be one of the first things we'll do.

It's starting to get a little dark now so I pull up my collar and walk faster. I clear the last of the foliage and see her again, very close. She hasn't seen me yet and she seems to have given up on walking around. She stands looking out over the water, visibly shaking. Her posture seems to indicate she has relinquished something – probably hope – and her fists open and close. It's time.

"Hey, Miss."

You'd think she'd received an electric shock. She jumps and turns towards me at the same time, and although she doesn't cry out, some low animal sound escapes her. Every muscle that isn't already tense winds right up and she lands in a half crouch. She looks as though she is ready for fight or flight. I figure it will be flight if I don't ease the tension somewhat. I hold up one hand, palm towards her.

"Miss, please. It's ok. I'm ok." This is actually true, but I don't think she believes me. If her eyes open any wider they'll fall out.

"Who… you…"

She's holding her own hands out now, trying to fend me off even though I'm yards away.

"I'm Dave. Just relax. I'm glad to see you. I'm a friend."

I've read that at times like this when folk are scared stiff and the subconscious is very close to the surface, they'll only hear the verbs and nouns. I'm therefore avoiding using words like 'harm' and 'danger'.

She looks past me and then back again. There is moisture in both eyes.

"All the people gone, where have they gone? I was with Mark and he just… he just went, and the other bloke in the bank. They just went, clothes… on floor. All people gone. Disappeared."

"Dissolved?" I want to describe it to her as I saw it – see if she agrees.

She nods.

"Yeah, yeah, dissolved. Did you see them go? Oh shit, where are they?"

She is close to panic again and I've got to move this forward or it's going to be dark and cold.

"Look Miss. I'm as confused as you and probably just as scared. At about 2.30pm this afternoon everyone I was with just faded away, in seconds. You're the only person

I've seen since then so for heaven's sake let's be friends, eh?"

She's not quite ready to settle down yet. I'll let her talk herself into it.

"The people in the cars just stopped and then…" (she uses our word of choice) "…dissolved. It's the bloody government or the army. Some experiment. I… Dave, yeah?"

I nod.

"Dave, have you seen anyone else. Is it just this town or what? I was going to try and drive but I can't. I was going to take my test but… Oh God I'm so scared"

This is a girl on the edge. Oh yes. About twenty five years, slim, brown hair and a small turned up nose. She's pretty, but she's lost all her reserve, the way she would normally hold herself. All poise is gone. In just a few short frantic hours most of the bonds and protocols of the twenty first century western woman have been stripped away. She's not strong. She's almost given up already. Or am I expecting too much? Let's make an appeal.

"Look love. What's your name? Let's be honest. There's just you and me as far as we know, at least for now. I'll walk away if you want. I'll go right now, but think. If I was a bad guy I could outrun you and overpower you. I'm not going to do either of those things. Some massive, weird… event has happened, and for some reason we can't guess at, you and I have survived. We can be together for a while… we can try and work it out… or we can be alone."

It's like we're trying to out-stare each other. I can see the internal dialogue going on behind her eyes, and God knows what she sees in mine.

"What do you say? Friends?"

There's a long pause and a thousand things happen behind her eyes... and then the tears come. Good. There are loud sobs. She takes a step forward and then back again, torn between lack of trust and the need to touch somebody. Good. Finally she runs and holds me, buries her head in my chest and cries her little heart out. I hold her gently and look out over the grey lake. There are still lights showing in the houses between the trees. The transmission grid will run between 6 and 18 hours with no intervention, and there is going to be none. We're on borrowed time already. We need to get somewhere else before the lights go out.

A heron glides by in the silence and settles on the dusky lake shore.

*****

We're three weeks in now and doing ok. I'm standing at the window of the old farmhouse peeling the last of the fresh oranges over the sink. The year has turned and there's an autumn blow going on outside. The wind pushes a gang of brown leaves onto the farm track, and they cross, like miniature schoolchildren in raincoats, tumbling. There are no more schoolchildren now I remind myself. School's out. World's out.

The girl's name is Monica. I knew that though from her name tag at the bank. It's funny though, I quite liked it pinned to her chest but I don't like it as a form of address. It sounds a bit common when she says it. She's not really what I was expecting. Mind you, she's thawed out somewhat and is actually beginning to be of some help. She still can't quite get her head round the fact that everyone else in the world has just gone and it makes her a little irrational sometimes – but I can't blame her for that. She wants to travel around and look for people – can't blame her for that either – but for now she accepts that we have to get ourselves a safe base and then make other plans.

I picked this farmhouse well. The wind turbine that the previous owner installed gives us light and the generator gives some heat. There's no shortage of petrol of course if you know how to siphon – and I do – and we've collected a fine array of motor cars. There's a Land Rover, a Porsche GT, and a small Volkswagen – that's for Monica's driving lessons, which aren't really going that well. I still feel drawn to the coast, but I think that's for next week. I still have to move things along a little bit yet.

The door opens and she comes in, windswept and mucky.

"The chickens haven't laid again. I can't work it out," she says. "Everything seemed fine and now they've stopped."

She lays the empty basket on the table and runs a hand through her hair.

"They're agitated for some reason – it's almost like they want to tell me something. Still, it won't worry you will it? You hate eggs."

Yes. I hate eggs. Monica doesn't. She likes eggs. Fried, boiled, scrambled. Eggs turn my stomach. But there are no eggs now.

"Yep, Monica. I still hate eggs. I'm the only guy in the world that hates eggs."

"That's not funny, Dave."

I try to look contrite. "Sorry, bad joke. There's probably a fox about, they can sense it. I'll get something out of a tin."

"Ok. I'll get cleaned up."

We've got separate rooms, of course. I haven't pushed things that far along yet. I did get a kiss and a hug last week when I'd finished chopping logs and fired up the wood burner. She backed off though, a little embarrassed at her recklessness. I was a perfect gentleman.

Monica is a modest girl, she always dresses to placate and not arouse. Again I can't blame her, stuck as she is, alone on a planet with a guy she doesn't know. We went shopping – well shoplifting – in town before we came out here. I thought she might take the chance to get some nice clothes, but no. All walking shoes and fleece tops, not an evening dress in sight. She's got to learn to enjoy this new world more…

Later we're sitting in candlelight over the remains of a steak pie. The wind whistles in the thatch and a hunter's moon troubles the shadows in the yard outside. Monica is fiddling with the transistor radio again, wasting yet another set of batteries on a sea of static. Every now and again she thinks she hears a glitch, the ghost of a transmission and pulls the radio to her ear.

"There's nothing there you know, love."

"But how do you know? How can you be so sure?"

I shrug. "I dunno. I just feel it."

"Then tell me, what's the shotgun for?"

I turn to the kitchen door and look at the weapon. She's right. What is it for?

"You're so negative for God's sake. How can we be the only people left?" She slams the radio down. "Dave, I've been thinking. Let's travel. Let's take the Land Rover and look. Tomorrow."

Her chin is stuck out, waiting for me to say no. Instead I smile.

"Ok. Tomorrow. You're right. We'll go to a couple of towns and then on to the coast. We'll see what state the place is in."

Those wide eyes again. "Really? No kidding?" It's almost a squeal. She taps her palms on the table excitedly. It's like a part of her wants to be rescued from a life alone with me. Of course it does.

"Yeah, why not. I guess this new world of ours should be a democracy, eh?"

I think I'm going to get another kiss, but I don't. She jumps up and does a little dance.

"Cool, cool. I'll pack some clothes. Let's go straight after breakfast." She heads for her room and then turns to look back. "Maybe there'll be some eggs. Goodnight, Dave."

I hear her bare feet on the stairs.

No. There'll be no eggs. I hate eggs.

★★★★★

We know what the shotgun is for now. There was a pack of dogs – all sorts – scratching and whining around the chicken run as we left this morning. They looked half starved. We tried to make it to the Land Rover unnoticed, but of course we didn't. They turned on us and Monica froze. I leaned forwards against the recoil, put both barrels into the leader and they scattered into the bushes. I reloaded and told her to get a towel but she just stood there panting. Useless. Ten minutes later and I'd wiped him off the side of the vehicle and we were on our way.

"C'mon buck up," I said, giving her a mock punch on the shoulder. "We're on a road trip. A picnic."

Her eyes were a little haunted.

"How can you be cheerful? They were going to rip us apart, and there'll be more."

I gave myself a bit of a smile.

"Maybe not."

★★★★★

It's a clear blue day as we stand on the cliffs. The bad weather has moved to the north and we're facing a fresh southwester. The air is beautiful. I'm a little disappointed there are no big wrecks to see. Still, I guess it's a numbers game, and if we walk enough of the coast… well maybe. There is one large vessel towards the horizon. It's not anchored and has moved visibly moved since we arrived, so I assume it's adrift. Monica became excited, thinking it was some kind of rescue. I'm afraid I burst her bubble and now she's mopey again.

There is one small touch that curiously affects me a little. There are two sets of clothes crumpled in the grass next to a hamper. Everything is sodden wet of course, and a little ragged now. We spend a thoughtful minute speculating on the owners last seconds on earth and Monica cries a little. From the way the sleeves are laid you could believe they were holding hands. I have to say I'm a little sad, for a while. I take Monica's hand, hoping for some response. She lays her head on my shoulder, and it suddenly occurs to me to level with her.

"My God, Dave, every time I think I'm getting used to this it all comes piling back into my head. Where ever they all went, why the hell didn't we? Why were we chosen to stay here and watch it all? I mean Christ, I work in a bank, and you, you're a journalist. Why us?"

Why indeed. I catch myself. Not yet. I put a hand around her and kiss her hair. She smells good today.

"Dave?"

"Yes, Monica?"

"I can't eat our picnic with those clothes there, and I can't bring myself to throw them over the cliff. Let's find another place."

"Nice hotel in town?"

She nods.

*****

We're quite drunk now. The bar at the Hotel La Manche is quite a grand affair, with its sweeping bay windows giving a wide view of the sea and its art deco furniture strewn around. We're into our second bottle of champagne and I've started on the whiskey. Monica has actually laughed a couple of times – proper laughter, proper, careless 'no problems in the world, damn it all' laughter. Her body language has changed completely and we've spent some time swopping anecdotes of the world before. She gave me a bit of a shock a while ago. I thought she was slipping off to the ladies room, but she returned from the gift shop wearing makeup, striking a pose and giving me a 'what do you think' look. I said I approved.

This is all very promising. This is what I'd hoped for.

She slumps on the sofa and pours us another drink.

"I bet you were a party girl," I venture.

She shrugs. "Maybe, sometimes."

I put my glass down. "Do you fancy a party now?"

I see a smile that I haven't seen before. This is how I imagined she might smile when I picked her. She places her glass next to mine, leans over and kisses me. I cup the back of her neck and rub it softly. She breaks off, breathes gently onto my face and I move her slowly backwards onto the sofa…

…Then there's a noise from the wide doorway. We both stop what we're doing and stare. A large white cat with four tiny kittens in tow moves cautiously into the room. It gives another plaintive meow and lies down while its offspring sniff the air and shuffle around it.

"Oh look, Dave. Look at them. They're lovely."

I feel my hackles rise.

"Christ, Monica, they're just bloody cats." I turn her face back to mine but she eases free and gets up.

"Monica!"

I'm forgotten. I won't be forgotten. Not now. We were

so close. I stare past her at the animals. She's holding her hand out and making small cute noises. I can feel a resentment taking over and a familiar wave washes over me. I feel my eyeballs roll up and I lie back heavily as the neurones begin to fire.

The webs are flooding as the linkages find each other. It's so easy now where it used to take so much effort. A few seconds later and then I'm done. I hear the strangest scream escape Monica, there's disbelief and a desperate fear contained within it. I open my eyes and look past her again just in time to see them go, becoming transparent, wafting away. Dissolving.

The bell on the collar gives a solitary 'tink' as it hits the carpet.

Monica is frozen for a few moments, and then her head slowly rotates towards me. There's that look again. Poise gone, eyes wide, mouth hanging open like a retard as she looks to me for some anchor against the chaos that is threatening to consume her.

I sigh.

"No, Monica. Don't ask. I don't know where they've gone."

And it's true, I really don't know where they've gone, the cats and the dogs and the eggs.

I don't know where the people have gone either. But I do know why they went there, every last sad stinking one of them, with their narrow prejudices and their dumb pride. All the stuck up neo right fascists, the doughy middle class mothers and the tattooed troglodytes. The mindless legions of the favoured west and the squalid east, all anchored to their shitty world views while a wild and wonderful universe sparked around them.

I sent them.

I've been sending things for most of my life.

It started when I was very young, as soon as I was self-aware really. I used to wish away the things that scared me – or that I didn't like. We all do it, except that with me they actually went, and they stayed gone. The biggest shock was finding out gradually that I was the only one who could do it. I reflect on it now, and I'm painfully glad that I only had limited ability early on, that I couldn't wish away the big things, bad babysitters, the bad people at school – the bringers of pain and sleepless nights. That would have led to discovery and trouble before I was ready. No, it was mostly flies, wasps and the like – and later on a small noisy dog. Only organic things for some reason, living tissue – the dentist's drill and the unwanted Christmas jumpers had to stay. Later on, in my teens I began to flex this strange muscle. I found out that once I had the 'pattern' of a thing – its template, I could duplicate the phenomena on all its fellows.

I decided to try a species

I researched something obscure and came up with some South American bug, well known to science and quite rare, but nowhere near extinction. I wanted to cause a fuss. It took most of the night, but eventually I did it, sweating from the effort and sleeping for ten solid hours afterwards. Then I waited for the news, scanning the science journals for months. Eventually I found it, just a small article. 'Scientists puzzled'. I bet. Fine work.

I can recall going into my 'state' for the first time consciously, eyes rolling up and the internal images popping into existence. I've never described it to anyone and I can't even rationalize it now. There are spider's webs but they're not spider's webs. It's a grid representation of the essence of something in my mind's eye, an organic frame. There are spiders but not spiders at the centre of each web. I must make them connect – join up and then pop. Their black juice, their filaments flood the webs and when they are all covered – it takes minutes now not hours – the thing I'm wishing is just gone.

Lost to the universe. Press control/delete.

I suppose someone more unbalanced, less possessed of themselves would have used this strange thing for gain, but you see I never did – well not much. I always felt I was saving it up for something really big, for a time when the world or some part of it needed punishing. Thirty five years and some bad decisions later and that time arrived about four weeks ago. The job went in the same week that cheating whore dropped her bombshell. I was drunk for the next few days, alone at home and stuck to the TV watching the news of the wars, the hate and the ruin. I sat night after night in my own stink listening to the fatuous drone of celebrity, the false words, and realising the obvious truth that we never learn a lesson from any single thing that happens.

First of all it was organised religion that was going to get it, then a random selection of tawdry world leaders, all to be gathered up in my strange head-net and sent to wherever. For a few brief moments it was actually going to be me that went (could I actually do that?), a strange suicide that would be, a banishment par excellence.

But no, I slowly realised that I was sick of them all. Not just everyone I knew but everyone that was. I can't say that I didn't deliberate somewhat, I even realised at some level that I might be sick, and that the sickness was making me think like this. But hey, I figured that you played the cards you were dealt, and I had a great hand. I then decided that I didn't want to face the rest of my life alone, and that's when my thoughts turned to the girl in the bank, gorgeous Monica. She was the chosen one.

I stayed in one Thursday about three weeks ago and lay on my bed concentrating. Strangely enough, laying my head grid down on the whole of humanity wasn't the hard part. It was excluding Monica from the great departure that took all the effort. It seemed I had to have her in my sights while everybody else went, to have some kind of connection with what I wanted to keep – hence my short vigil outside the windows of the bank and subsequent walk to the lake as she wandered in panic.

It seemed the universe gave a great sigh as they went. I felt a huge pressure release inside me as seven billion souls shed their rags and drifted away.

Now of course it's all gone wrong.

Monica continues to stare at me for a few seconds, and then she gives a weird shrug and puts her hands to her chest. She's trying to say something to me but she has no breath to speak with. There's a different kind of shock in her eyes now, a sharp fear. It's a heart attack. A massive cardiac event I figure, and I just stand there not believing how unlucky I am as she falls to the floor. Eventually I prod myself into action, and I mess about for a while with 'rescue breathing', CPR, whatever. It's all to no avail. The poor girl is limp pale and cold, not attractive at all, and I am truly alone.

*****

We're having a bit of a cuddle now and I'm watching the sun go down over the sea. Monica's skin is very cold, but the whiskey is insulating me somewhat. I have of course decided on a course of action – the only one really. I'm going to find out where they've all gone, all the people, the bugs and eggs and dogs and cats. It's just a great pity that Monica won't be there, *she*, after all, took a more conventional way out.

I close my eyes and search. Ah, there I am – a small web in the middle of my mind's eye. It's starting to flood, black and thick, and as it finishes, closing in on itself, I feel a lifting, a lightening. There's a whoosh – more felt than heard – and I'm standing, no floating, in a vast grey place. It seems the very air is opaque, and there are shapes moving within it. I look a bit harder. They're coming towards me now.

All of them.

EIGHT

The fat man drives west at speed and the sun rises behind him. It shortens the shadows and gives colour to the rocky bluffs and sparse vegetation. He has left the city far behind, stewing in the August night. He has left the dirty hotel owing money and with most of his clothes strewn around the room. He has no fear of his inevitable discovery, and is only concerned by the possibility of being stopped before he is finished.

He has left the child's body in a dumpster on the edge of town. He is almost done.

The man wipes sweat from his eyes and shoots a look at the fuel gauge. He will make it to the city easy enough if the rest of the car holds together. It was a quick and anonymous purchase, and he hadn't expected it to last this long. Maybe it will see him to the end. He is almost done.

Herman Cody has killed and dumped six children, one a week for six weeks. Five bodies have been found and the news networks are drooling. Daily bulletins trawl anguished faces of parents and siblings. Officers of the law, state and federal, talk of the net closing and make their appeals for vigilance. All the children have been knifed and mutilated, and a few scant details released to stoke the national outrage. Herman doesn't listen or watch. He must feed his condition. He must focus, just two to go.

At eleven a.m. he turns off the engine in the car park of a mall on the edge of town. A small amount of steam issues from the hood and Herman imagines the vehicle is sighing as it senses the end. He feels that child number seven is near and wonders if it feels safe, if it feels him nearby. He wonders if it feels his lust, his need.

'Think of it as a game, Hermancody.'

He lifts his bulk from the car on stiff muscles and stretches against the open door. The heat almost chokes him and the dirty shirt sticks where it touches, which is everywhere. He yawns and scans the car park fighting desperation and fatigue.

'You're close,' he thinks. 'You're very close my poor dead baby.'

Families cross the lot with trolleys containing groceries and children. There are cries for ice cream or soda. There is laughter and frustration. There are exhaust fumes and music. Here is America, unsuspecting and vulnerable.

Herman feels a sudden and familiar tug at the front of his head. The beacon has been a gift, part of the game, a tool. He turns his head to where he is bidden. A family is crossing the lot with a full trolley. Father is pushing, salt and pepper hair cut short, pale blue shirt and chinos. A country club man. Mother is thirtyish and fey. Her blond hair is careless but planned to perfection and she wears a summer dress that touches where it should. A dutiful but independent woman. They are perfect and Herman knows that they are happy, for now. Two children orbit; a boy about six or seven clutching an action figure, and a girl, as blond as mom, who skips around in defiance of the heat.

37

Not the boy. The girl. She is number seven.

They pass close by on their way to the car. Country club guy offers Herman a quick glance and an unconscious wrinkle of the nose. The glance speaks volumes.

'You fat smelly fuck,' it says, 'look at my life.'

Herman holds his eyes for a brief moment.

'Yes I am,' he thinks. 'As for your life, I'm going to take most of it away. I don't wanna, but I gotta. It's getting to the end you see. I can even be careless. There's just one more after yours.'

Hours later, as night takes the desert again, he has indeed been careless. Just a straight march to their front door and an urgent knock. Dad answers and is taken down with a tyre iron. Herman strides through the house to the kitchen. Blond mom is in a dressing gown and she gets the same. He meets the girl on the stairs and stifles a scream with his large dirty hand, scooping her up and hurrying over the lawn to his car. She wets herself and then passes out in his arms.

'You're kidding no one,' he thinks and throws her in the back.

Soon the protesting vehicle has taken them from the suburbs and into yet another vacant lot. A warm wind is pushing trash around and two ragged dogs shine their eyes into the headlights before scampering off.

'I'm a dog too,' thinks Herman, 'just a lost ragged dog.'
'Take them at night and don't ask why'.

The girl begins to stir. Herman eases around with difficulty, clutching the hunting knife he keeps in the glove box. He has the long plastic gloves on now. They disassociate him in some small way, depersonalising the deed. Her eyes become saucers and she begins to kick. He closes his fat fingers around her throat and stops a scream.

"Look at me girl." She is unlikely to do anything else. "Show me what you are before I do this."

Their eyes meet, but all he sees is a little girl, beyond fright, and for a moment he falters…

"Show me!"

She brings her lids down slowly, and in the instant before the eyes are lost there is something else.

"That's enough, honey."

Herman lunges with the knife and is very soon done. The car has to go now. There is blood everywhere. He pulls her head forward and exposes the back of her neck. There it is. A quick scoop and twist and he has it. Breathing heavily he takes the plastic bag from the glove box and places his trophy with the other six.

All his strength now leaves him. He feels filthy and tired beyond words. He removes his gloves and rubs his eyes. He won't even bother to hide this one. His wallet holds three hundred dollars, that's enough for the time he has left. He can already feel a pull in his head. Number eight is close. Herman doesn't know if this is luck or design and isn't much bothered.

Five minutes later and he is shuffling through dark streets shouldering the duffle bag containing the knife, plastic bag and not much else. The old car is burning, cracking and popping its last, and already there are sirens on the hot wind.

*****

Deputy Murphy is shaking and the sweat is stinging his eyes as he stares down the barrel. Yet he mustn't blink, mustn't move. He feels somehow that this is his moment. About three minutes ago the fat guy had appeared from the drugstore, making no attempt to hide his intention, waddling, with kid in one hand and a knife in the other. Murphy's radio lies where he had dropped it after calling it in. There are still screams but the street has mostly cleared.

"I'm telling you again, sir, let go the boy. We'll work it out."

That's it, Murphy, talk him down. That's what they tell you.

Now there are sirens, many and close. Thank God. The guy is leaning against the wall at the entrance to the alley next to the pharmacy. He is obviously in some distress and is clutching the young boy like a talisman, the big knife at his throat. He keeps shaking his head and Murphy believes he is crying.

"Sir, can you hear that? This is going to get a lot worse soon. Let the boy run to me."

He thinks the boy is curiously calm, and seems to be looking from Murphy to his captor. Waiting. Amused? No, in shock. That's it, shock.

"Leave me, officer. Just leave me. I've gotta do this. This is the last one."

'There will be eight children.'

Last one. Christ it can't be him. Murphy's chest

tightens. This is the Interstate Knifeman. This is him, on my watch.

"Sir… just… please…"

Brakes squeal, there are shouted commands and the cicada chatter of twenty or more guns being cocked. A hand is on his shoulder.

"What's he said, Murphy?"

"He… he says he's got to do it. This is the guy. The fucking interstate guy."

Murphy watches as the fat guy looks around in desperation. The black kid is still silent. Suddenly the child is shaken violently and held at arm's length. Mister, that's a big mistake you just made. The guy is holding the boy as far from him as he can. Murphy lowers his gun. He doesn't want this to be his moment. He knows everyone just took aim.

The guy shouts, angry and hoarse.

"You see this? What do you think this is? A kid? A little boy? It ain't. It… It's something else. I… I was chosen… I got something here you gotta see, in this bag."

He reaches awkwardly behind him with his knife hand and produces what looks like a small plastic bag.

'Why you, Hermancody?'

"Look. Please look!"

Then the kid just takes one strange exaggerated step to the side and exposes the man. The guy drops the bag and begins to swing with the knife. There are four shots that burst his shirt and push him back into the wall. He falls like a sack.

Two hours later and the heat is coming off the day. The

crime scene is intact and Murphy guards it as the forensics crawl and prod. The ambulances have left with their charges, the knifeman to the morgue and the kid to wherever they take kids who have been through this. Next to the chalk outline of the killer (jeez that was one fat guy) is another that circled the small plastic bag. That has gone too now, but Murphy saw them examine it, and still feels a little nauseous.

"What the hell? Slugs."

"Slugs? Get out of here."

"Really. Slugs. But small, and kinda blue."

"Weird. Bag 'em."

"They're in a bag."

"Well bag the bag, Randall. Bag the bag."

★★★★★

After the doctor leaves the room, David and his parents sit in silence for a while. Dolories rocks her son in her arms.

"Mom, is the guy dead?"

"He sure is my darling. He can't hurt you no more."

★★★★★

'Why you, Hermancody? Why not? You are random, as are we. Think of it as a game Herman, for that is what it is for us. We are very old and never tire of such amusements. Don't try to use logic, we've done this before many times over many ages and with many of your people. This time there will be eight children and they will all be within a thousand mile radius of your home. Of

course they won't be children, not any more. They will be us. Take them at night and don't ask why. You will hunt us and kill the child we inhabit. You will take a trophy from each one of us. Eight trophies and you will be done. Then we will withdraw, at least for a while – we certainly won't trouble you again, my friend. We will give you the capacity to detect us from a distance and we will behave as these children would. We will not make your hunt easy or hard. We will simply be. It's a challenge, you see. Can you become a monster in the eyes of your people? Can you break every instinct and convention in order to save these same people? Can you go to your grave knowing that the world will revile your memory and your name? You had better hope the answer is yes, my friend. The prize for success is a stay of execution for this sorry world, until we choose to play again. The price of failure is extinction. This is our game you see – our curiosity.'

'So, Hermancody, do you hunt or does everybody die?'

She holds his head between her palms and looks into his eyes as he closes them. Just at the moment they close she gives a little gasp and lets him go…

THE ARCHER OF
BROKEN PINE TOR

Once there was a man named Frederick Alarcy who lived and died. He left a widow and two strong sons, and they lived through their grief on the slopes of Broken Pine Tor, close to where the great waterfall hits the Darwin River and the place where the deer come to drink.

They did not want for pity or help, as Frederick Alarcy had been an honest and respected man. By summer's end the crops were in, the firewood put by, and people's minds turned to other things. Widow Alarcy was a fair woman, and soon found the attention of some of the local men. They came from the town on the night of the first snow and asked for shelter.

"But you have your own homes," said the widow from behind the door, waving her sons to silence.

"Yes, but we would have some comfort from the heat of the wood we helped to lay in," one replied.

"I hear you, Benjamin Resker, but your own wife will be waiting with your girls. Warm yourself by your own fire, and take my gratitude with you, for this wood is dry and burns well."

This did not satisfy them, for they were worse for drink, and pushed into the small house without the caution of sobriety. They made free with dead Alarcy's beer and spirits, and with his wife. They left the widow tearful and clutching her sons to her chest, and the door swinging in the first swell of a winter gale.

The snows came and went, and with them the widow's hope, for she was heavy with a child. The boy arrived in high summer, and was named Thomas. Through custom he could not take the name Alarcy, for he was, as the people said, a child of force, and although he was not outcast, he was shunned, both by his half-brothers and the people of the town. As time passed, he was educated not in the school, but by Old Madam Foxmere, the cunning woman from the wood above the great waterfall. She took the slow ones and the lost ones and made of them what she could. The children of the town learned high words and history, while Thomas learned with his hands the ways of the wood and of the earth. His words were few, both to his mother, who gave him what love she could, and to others, who were happy for him to pass in silence.

He went far into himself, and learnt focus, being able to concentrate for hours on the smallest thing. He learnt from the old woman that a man may have a purpose even though others would deny him one. He made catapults and slings from the deadfall and vine and cultivated a sure eye, though unlike the other children, his targets were not the birds or the small scurrying things, but blankets stuffed with straw made into effigies of men. These he struck without error or hesitation, and their fabric became ragged with the scars of many sharp stones.

In his seventeenth year, Thomas' name was put

forward for the war lottery. Many assured his mother that
this was the best future for a child of force, and that even
though the boy's life could never serve a true purpose, at
least he could show his family some honour. The widow
Alarcy cried many tears, and his half-brothers shared a
smile as Thomas' name was pulled from the drum by the
recruiting Sergeant. Thomas, focused and silent, stepped
forward to acknowledge, and without turning, walked
slowly to join the line of the chosen.

The march to the barracks took them past the woods,
and past Old Mother Foxmere who sat in the shade of an
oak, whittling. As Thomas drew level she stood stiffly and
matched his pace.

"Take this as a gift, Thomas, and find your purpose."

She handed him an arrow, straight and true, carved
from ash with a flame hardened point and with crow
feathers for its flight. Thomas nodded without a word. He
tucked the arrow into his shoulder bag and walked away
from the town forever.

★★★★★

Their training was hard and short, for the war would not
wait. It had held the two nations in its bloody grip for
many years, and the disputed borderland, the origin of the
conflict, was laid waste. Horse, sabre, cannon round and
bullet were the only shared dialogue, and their daily
exchange fuelled the need for endless sacrifice.

Thomas fared better than most at the barracks. Where
others complained at the hardship and discipline, he

embraced it. Where they took their comfort in comradeship, he rejected it, content to be alone and without purpose, focus his only friend. His sure hand and eye brought him to the attention of the rifle masters, who pressed him to join their ranks as a sharpshooter. He asked instead to join the company of archers, preferring the form and silence of the bow. It called to him of the trees and earth, of the spirit of the forest. Once again he attracted scorn, for his choice of weapon was an uncommon one.

He was however called to the ranges one morning, and the Master Bowman addressed him haughtily.

"This is not a weapon of mass slaughter boy, but of surgery. The company of archers plough a lonely path. We are assassins and approach our targets as a cat stalks. Each bowman travels with just his marker for company. One arrow must suffice, for then you are discovered and must retreat to hiding. Few have a natural skill that I can develop."

Thomas met his eye, and without a word strode forward, picking and weighing a bow in one fluid movement. He withdrew three arrows from a leather quiver, stuck each in the ground, and spun towards the targets that stood across the range. Releasing a slow breath, his focus took him and he loosed all three arrows in twice that number of seconds. All struck true in the red stain at the centre of the farthest target. He shouldered the bow and once again met the master's eye.

The man reached out and lifted Thomas' chin.

"What do they call you, boy?"

"They generally call me nothing, sir. But I am Thomas of Broken Pine Tor and I have no purpose."

The man nodded slowly.

"Well you do now."

★★★★★

So Thomas took the green and grey of the company. He was teamed with a marker called Rafe Feasley, a slight man with whom he shared a mutual dislike. Rafe prized his spyglass as Thomas prized his bow, and together they served in forest and field, taking missions as they came. Here, a General of the opposition, visiting the forward lines; there, an enemy sharpshooter who had wreaked havoc all summer long amongst their cannon crew, and many others. Thomas never missed, and his reputation grew, along with the envy of his fellows. Once again he stood apart.

One cold autumn dawn, they lay hid amongst the ferns at the top of a wooded ridge. Rafe, propped on his elbows, held his spyglass steady and scanned the village that hugged the bottom of the hill. The village, though belonging to the other side, had recently been occupied and looted by their troops. Food was short at the front, and the infantry ill-disciplined and hungry. Shouts of protest reached their ears as the troops moved from house to house, demanding provisions and making rough work of those that argued. Rafe focused on the meeting hall, occupied by the officer corp. Their intelligence had told of a dignitary from the government who would visit that morning, and would serve as their prey. The marker's breath condensed in the freezing air as he moved the focus wheel.

"Cover your mouth, Rafe Feasley, your breath will reveal us."

"Mind your own mouth, archer. It is your talent for death that has us here in the first place, and not around the breakfast pot with our fellows."

Thomas made no reply, but regarded the town with his own keen eyes. A commotion arose louder than the rest, and a group of infantry poured from one of the thatched houses dragging a woman. Her cries and their laughter cut the morning.

"See what you get now, you sow? We'll take your food and we'll take this."

Two of them threw her roughly across a barrel, as the others, swigging their loot, circled around. The ringleader ripped her top and spread her legs. Thomas tensed and began to rise, but Rafe took his arm.

"Look there!"

Two black horses pulled a carriage into view around the corner of the meeting hall. They pulled up at the door amidst a flustered ceremony and standing to attention.

"It's him, bowman." He raised the glass again. "He will be out in a moment. Be quick and sure."

Thomas had already appraised the scene, but turned back to regard the struggling woman.

"Bowman! On my life, she is a peasant and probably deserves her lot. Let them have their force, she will beg for more when they are done, and maybe they will give her a strong and arrogant son like you."

He kicked out and struck Thomas in the shin. Below, a fat man in the purple uniform of government office stepped from the carriage with the aid of a footman. Thomas stood, glancing from one to the other. Rafe's cheeks reddened with fury, and he hissed.

"For God's sake, you forced scum. Find your focus. Who do you think you are?"

Thomas lowered his eyes to the man while reaching back to his quiver. He spoke quietly.

"I am Thomas of Broken Pine Tor. I have my focus, and I have my purpose."

In a blur he bent his knees and loosed his first arrow. The dawn air hissed and the government man fell dead. The second was drawn and found its target in Rafe's left eye. He died gasping. Thomas now took one step forward and broke cover. Five more arrows followed and five of the drunken infantry hit the cobbles amidst broken glass and spilt beer. The woman's screams died in her throat as her aggressor withdrew and clutched at his pants, turning around, agape.

Thomas reached into the quiver once more. His hand closed on yet another arrow. This one however, had not been turned and straightened by some military fletcher's hand. It was whittled from the wood of his native forest, with a flame blackened tip and crow's feathers for flight.

As he watched, the panicked infantryman drew the struggling, half naked woman in front of him, crouching behind her and staring wildly around. Shouts arose from the meeting hall as physik doctors rushed to tend the dignitary. Shots rang out and cracked the branches behind Thomas. He stood still. The soldier's upper body was barely visible now, an improbable shot at too long a distance. Thomas drew three long breaths as more bullets strafed the hillside.

His focus descended once more and wrapped itself around him, guiding his eye and hands. The arrow whistled as it flew, as if eager for the icy air and freedom. It entered the soldier's neck, and he slid to the ground as his life bled away.

The woman ran.

Thomas of Broken Pine Tor shouldered his bow, turned and strode quietly through the bracken. His green and grey met the colours of the forest. They took him and swallowed him, allowing him to share space with all the things that scurried and ran there, and to share its secrets and its darkness.

THE SCENT OF ELSEWHERE

November 1643

Darkest night.

Sheets of rain descend on the thatch of the inn and seek to breach its ancient barrier. Most of the water is carried down the slope and splashes on the stone and mud below. Some however finds gaps in the woven reed and forms into rivulets that twist as they descend. They steer an erratic course to penetrate through to the room below.

The pretty girl hitches up her skirt and moves from behind the bar carrying a bucket to catch the latest of many such intrusions. One thin stream falls from the thatch and finds an oak beam. It drips suddenly onto the back of a small mouse that shakes itself and scurries along the beam to a more secure perch. The creature's bright eyes regard the scene below and its nose twitches as it peers through the candlelight and studies the old man.

Leaning forward over the table and hugging his beer, the man is watching the girl as she returns to the bar. She runs a wet hand through her long hair, and raises her chin to the newcomer, wordlessly asking his pleasure. The old man sets his dark and hungry thoughts aside for a moment and switches his gaze to the man at the bar. This man is fresh from the storm outside, his black cloak drips onto the flags at his feet, the candles still flicker from his passing, and the iron handle of the heavy door still swings from recent use. He regards the girl through matted hair.

"Your best ale."

The smile doesn't reach her eyes.

"There's just one," she takes a tankard and pulls on a pump, "and this is it."

This forces a laugh from the other two occupants of the inn. Two farmers deep in the shadows at the far side of the room, look up from their cards.

"You tell him, Rosamund."

The stranger turns slowly and nods to the men.

"I'm told." They return to their game.

The stranger throws two coins onto the bar and takes a drink. He studies his tankard for a moment.

"That'll do fine. Rosamund."

"Hmph." The girl spins around, grabs a cloth and sets to polishing a line of tankards. Across the room the old man stirs. He rubs his eyes, and when he speaks his voice is gravel.

"You may not believe this stranger, but that's a better reception than most get." He laughs from the throat and it turns into a wet cough. The stranger turns and leans back onto the bar, he gestures to the door.

"It's a better reception than this bleak night has given me so far." The old man's eyes follow his gesture and he nods wordlessly, then…

"Bleak indeed, have you wandered far, stranger?"

The man looks at him and tilts his head.

"Wandered?"

"Why yes. I heard no hooves and heard no request for

stabling, and…" He gestures with his flagon. "Those boots suit a walking man."

The stranger regards him for a moment with a hard stare. Then he grins.

"Yes, old man. Far."

A new sound rises over the hiss of the rain. The clatter of horseshoes on a wet stone road. The sound increases and causes all those inside to stop whatever they are doing. The stranger and the old man hold each other's gaze, frozen. The girl holds her position and her breath – one hand is holding the cloth buried deep in a glass – and the two card players turn to the nearest window although there is nothing but the night visible without. As the riders pass, each bottle along the shelf behind the bar chinks against its neighbour and their contents ripple. Abruptly the sound is gone and the hiss of rain resumes. The stranger takes a swig of his beer and speaks to the door.

"The King's men. That was a disciplined troop."

The old man nods slowly but then stops.

"Or the Wild Hunt."

"The Wild Hunt?"

"Aye, the Lord of Faerie sends his riders abroad on nights such as – "

"I know what the Wild Hunt is, old fellow, and I know that it is a tale for children."

He turns back to the bar and holds his tankard out the girl.

"I knew that I had wandered far from the town, but I didn't realise I had wandered so far from reason."

"Hah!" This from one of the farmers.

The girl takes his tankard and fills it, holding his stare. She seems to have softened somewhat and gives him a smile.

"Don't mind old Thomas, stranger, he'll wear you away with his stories. Many are the paying customers who have walked out that door on worse nights than this rather than hear his babble."

The stranger takes his beer.

"Is that right, Thomas? Are you bad for trade? Well, I'll not be forced out. I've come too far and I'm too cold. Maybe we'll have a story or two, eh?

Thomas raises his eyes, unsure if he is being mocked. The barmaid shakes her head.

"I warn you, sir"

The stranger waves her away and moves to sit opposite the old man. He touches their tankards together and the candle between them flickers as if excited.

"Well, Thomas, the Wild Hunt was it? What other tales of Faerie do you have? It seems like the night for it and I have nothing but time."

Thomas hugs his beer again and grunts.

"I think you would make fun of me, sir. Have you come from the town to amuse yourself with the likes of us tonight? If so I will give you no such entertainment…"

Then he leans forward and his voice softens. There are discoloured teeth within his sly smile.

"…if however your interest is genuine, then I have something to tell. I know why the Wild Hunt rides."

Above him, still peering down from the oak beam, the small mouse shakes itself. It has tired of the smoky room and the sounds it cannot understand. There are babies waiting for its milk and it needs the warmth of the nest. As it turns to run home a shadow falls. The cat has approached silently and is crouching low on the beam, tense and ready. The mouse gives one shrill scream as the predator's claws rip its life away.

Old Thomas looks up briefly but sees nothing. Then, fixing the other man's eyes, he begins.

"Now, as you probably know, the land of Faerie wraps around our world like a cloak – like your cloak. It exists within and without, all around us but distant. The fair folk can travel to us but we cannot travel to them, leastways not unbidden."

He looks past his companion to the girl, and then to the card players. All are apparently ignoring him, and the stranger knows they must have heard all this many times, but he senses they are listening.

"Their land is wondrous to us, more beautiful than we can imagine. They are beings of light, immortal, and terrible as they are mischievous. There are towers of gold and valleys of – "

"Just a minute, old Thomas. If they are so… wondrous, why bother with us at all? Why not ignore this mundane realm of rain and sadness?"

"Ah well, young man. They have a fascination with our kind you see, always have. They cannot understand our short lives or our… our weight. For all their glory, we have feelings that they don't possess. We are somehow deeper. They study us." He leans back and takes a deep drink. "Yes, that's it. They study us."

"What? Such as a doctor of Physic may study a caged rat?"

"Aye, yes sir, a caged rat. Then there is the sport."

A sharp gust of wind beats at the windows and the heavy door creaks above the sound of the storm. All within turn their eyes there for a moment. The stranger turns back.

"Ah yes, the sport, the Wild Hunt. I have heard the Faerie Lord sends his knights forth to roam our world on nights such as this. They hunt the white stag which is so dear to him, yet they never catch it."

The old man's eyes widen.

"Ah, so you have a little country knowledge within you."

"I have heard little boys' tales if that's what you mean, but that's all they are, and I fear this is just another, though I am no child, Thomas. I think it's time for me to go back to the barmaid, for she is prettier than you and I must arrange lodging."

He makes to stand, but the old man grabs a fold of his cloak and pulls him back.

"No, sir, it's not what you think. True the tales are often told, but they're told wrong. The stag is not what they hunt. Not mostly anyways."

The man sits back down and narrows his eyes.

"Oh no? So what is it they hunt?"

Now there is a lull in the wind and rain, for one brief moment something approaching silence inhabits the inn. When old Thomas speaks his voice is as a hiss.

"They hunt the lost."

The storm resumes.

"The lost? What are the lost?"

"Not what, sir. Who. The lost maidens of Faerie, those who have chosen to leave the realm behind. Those whose fascination with mortal man is so great they have passed into our world to live amongst us as ordinary girls and women. They have sacrificed all the long ages of eternity to burn brightly and briefly among us. Their wings fade and wither, as does most of their magic. They are... they are as we are."

The stranger tilts his head, his interest sparked again.

"And they live amongst us?"

"Yes sir, they work our fields, they whore our towns, and they serve our noble ladies. Some of them even *are* our noble ladies."

"You speak nonsense, old fella. Interesting nonsense I grant but nonsense nevertheless. If such a world existed, and if such beings lived within it, why would they possibly relinquish all that for..." he gestures around, "for this?"

He turns and sees Rosamund leaning on the bar, clearly intent on the story but scratching at the wooden surface and feigning disinterest.

"No offence to your fine inn, my girl."

"Well it's keeping you dry tonight, friend. Shall I make up a room?"

He nods. "Aye. Do that."

She gives him a playful smile that maybe has more within it, and leaves through the door behind the bar. He regards Thomas who now has his arms crossed.

"So the Lord, he seeks them out?"

"Yes, sir, he does. He is a jealous lord, and the realm of Faerie will not give up its own kind easily."

"So he sends out his hunt to fetch them back?"

"No, there is no return to glory for them. They are hunted and killed. They have relinquished their immortality, and they are truly shown what this means. It is said that in the last moment of their lives they regain their light and become for a moment what they once were." He takes a drink and wipes his lips. "Then they fade to dust, as must we. The fair folk call them 'Tinks', and they are lower to them than vermin."

"Hah! Tinks." His companion bangs his tankard down. "What a story you tell. I have never heard this, and I doubt that it has reached the ears of children either, or they would never sleep again."

"That's true, my friend, and yet there is more."

"More you say? Speak on, old Thomas!"

The girl returns and nods.

"There is a room at the end ready for you when you've drunk enough ale and heard enough nonsense."

"Room, yes. Beer, yes!" The stranger raises his tankard, apparently feeling the effects of the strong drink on an empty stomach.

"Let's have some more over here, and one for my tale weaving friend."

She takes their tankards away and begins to fill them. He turns back to the old man.

"So. More."

"Well. The Wild Hunt is a ruse sir. They are fairy folk

and believe it or not, ill-suited to killing their own kind. There are other kinds of hunter."

"Other kinds?"

"Yes, and we must not speak of them lightly young man, for they are as deadly to us as they are to any former maid of Faerie."

He leans forward and speaks in a whisper. The younger man mirrors him irreverently.

"The Faerie lord hires assassins, mortal men to seek out these women. They are hunters, mercenaries who can move through this world of ours more easily than those from beyond. They work for Faerie gold and the promise of long life. They are mongrels, sir, vicious dogs who kill without mercy."

"And how do they find these girls?"

"Ahh, you see. There's a scent, a sweet odour they can't quite rid themselves of. It's said to be quite wonderful and can make a man dream himself away. It's said to be the smell of the meadows and vales of the otherworld. The hunters are trained to detect it. They are given a small amount of magic to sharpen their senses. Although mortal in almost every way, the lost maidens cannot hide their true selves and it gives them away."

"So they are found, and killed, but how?"

"Well how do you think?"

"Er... Strangled with silk? Thrown under horses?" The stranger is clearly enjoying the chance to involve himself in the tale. "I know! They are made to listen to Old Thomas night after night. At the end of a week they take their own lives willingly. Ha!"

Thomas shakes his head although he is smiling. The stranger turns to see if the others are sharing in his joke. Rosamund stands at the bar with her hands on her hips, their full tankards foaming and ready.

"Ah, sweet Rosamund. Bring us the ale!"

"And have you lost the use of your legs?"

"Nearly, girl. The beer is stronger than I'm used to. Soon I'll be good for nothing."

Mischief creeps into her eyes.

"Nothing? Well that won't do." She hefts the tankards and brings them to the table. He gives her four coins and winks.

"This'll be the last, eh?"

She raises her eyes and moves over to the farmers who are also waving their empty tankards. He pushes Thomas' drink towards him and gestures.

"So. How are they killed?"

"Why, with iron, sir, an iron sword or dagger, an iron spear or even a pin."

His companion's eyes widen. "Yes! Of course. Iron is fatal to the fair folk. I have heard this. Just a graze or a scratch."

"Yes sir, or of course a thrust to the heart. They fear the metal above all else, and it is one part of their heritage these lost girls can never leave behind. They must beware it all their days on earth."

"So who are these men, are they known in our world?"

"Why yes, sir. Their names slip in and out of stories and legends, some are forgotten and some are thought of as pirates, warriors, highwaymen and bandits, but that is

61

not what they are. I will give you one name and you can tell me if it is familiar. Caleb Blackmoor."

The stranger narrows his eyes and rubs his forehead. His hand pauses there.

"Why yes. I have heard this name. A captain of our king turned robber. Parchments were up all over the town some time ago. A wanted man. A feared man."

"Aye. Feared. Feared by them above all." Old Thomas sits up straight on his bench. For a moment some of his years seemed to slip away, and a poise, a gravity, comes to his features.

"I, you see, was also a captain of the king for many years. I fought and I was feared."

He winks and uncertainty stirs in the other's eyes. The old man stands slowly. He is taller than the stranger has imagined, and stronger. There is nothing of the frail vagrant about him now. A chink of metal reveals a sword hung at his belt, and on his buckle the King's crest.

"Are you… are you he? Is this why you tell me this tale? Must I fear you?"

The farmers' muted conversation has stopped and the younger man feels their eyes at his back. For a moment there is just the rain and the wind. Then one of the farmers bursts into laughter. Rosamund squeals and bangs the bar, giggling. Thomas' shoulder slump.

"No, young sir. You must not fear me. I'm just a sad old soldier, a teller of tales who needs a piss."

He shuffles from behind the bench and limps towards the door by the bar. The stranger lets his breath go and turns to face the others. They are still laughing and he holds up his hands.

"Alright, alright. I am taken for a fool. It was a fine tale and I was convinced. I am glad to have been your entertainment on this bleak night."

With a tilt of their heads the two card players raise their glasses and Rosamund makes a shallow curtsey. He turns back unsteadily to his beer.

"Rosamund, girl! Look here! What's this? There's half a rats tail in my rutting ale."

Her smile disappears and she walks over to him as he gestures to the tankard on the table. As she draws next to him his eyes suddenly clear and he stiffens, all intoxication gone. In one swift and fluid move he reaches behind her head and draws a short iron sword from under his cloak. Both pulling and pushing, he drives the bright blade under her ribs and up into her beating Faerie heart. Hot golden blood pours over his hand as the girl shudders and shakes, held firm by his arm. Her eyes meet his with an expression of profound surprise and loss, and her last warm breath breaks on his cheek.

Now Thomas enters the room again. The shadows are dancing as the candles wave and stutter in some unfelt breeze. In that moment he sees something his stories have not prepared him for. He sees the back of the girl's blouse move as she slumps over the stranger's blade. It heaves once and her wings burst through the cloth, casting it aside. For one brief moment they spread and flap, gossamer thin and peacock bright, before they dry and fade to bracken. Her skin likewise glows with an ivory light, and her eyes, as they hold the stranger's shine green and bright.

Then all her life and long ages blink out, and she dies with a short sigh.

The man pushes her roughly away and withdraws his sword. She crumples and he bends to wipe the blade on her blouse. As he stands he meets Thomas' gaze. The old man is frozen to the spot, his mouth works to form words and his shaking hand gestures to the limp body on the floor.

"R…osy. You killed…"

The other forces a grim smile. "Don't weep for her, mate. She's just a dead 'Tink', turncoat scum. She fancied a mortal life…" He shrugs, "…and that's what she got. They all kiss the iron in the end. We see to that." He gestures to the bar. "I smelled her as soon as I came in. She had the scent about her." He nods to himself. "It really is beautiful."

Now Thomas points at him, the finger shaking violently. "Who… Who are you, and what are you about stranger?"

"I'm Caleb Blackmoor. I kill Faeries for gold."

He spins quickly and his cloak billows as his blade is sheathed. Moments later the old door bangs shut behind him and every candle is extinguished by the blast of cold wet air he has let in. The two farmers are frozen in place, rendered as statues by what they have seen. In the gloom, Thomas can barely see the girl's body limp on the stone floor.

In the warm thatch above them, a nest of blind young

mice squeal for their mother's milk. Their pink and hairless bodies crawl over each other in the darkness. The cat turns slowly at their mewling and quietly slinks, with menace and grace, along the beam.

ECHO VALLEY

I live in Echo Valley – I have done for some months now. Through days spent listening to the wind shake the winter trees or watching the same wind stroke the grass on far fields during a baking summer, I've almost seen the seasons round. Now autumn has come, and red and gold flank the valley as it widens to the west, opening to the beginnings of a sunset. I can see Jones and his dogs move the sheep through the fields some distance away, and his obscure calls, passed through the generations, move the animals in slow waves towards his farm. There are a thousand sights and sounds around me as I stand on the porch. They're becoming familiar as the months pass, but they also remain new. They have no relationship with the sights and sounds of the city.

I lived in the city you see. Then Jane died and I came here.

Behind me the house creaks and breathes as the boiler cuts in. I get a beer from the kitchen and sit heavily in the rocker to watch the end of the day approach. I run my hand over the rough wood of the porch and reflect again how much I love this place. It's old, a bit of a wreck and it's lonely like me, but it was a steal. Vacant for some years and nestled on the side of a hidden valley in the Welsh borderlands, it was easy to buy. Now it's easy to live in. We ask nothing of each other, and we gladly share each other's space.

Sound carries strangely here, further than it should. That's the reason I can hear Jones and his sheep now. He had explained this phenomenon to me some weeks ago when he called by with the firewood. We had finished unloading and stood by the woodpile breathing heavily. Cowbells broke the silence.

"Where's that coming from?"

"Ah them, that's Dafyd's herd down the way, he's taking them to milk." He'd gestured expansively to the west.

"But his farm is beyond yours, how can that be?"

Jones had pushed his flat cap back on his head and begun to roll a cigarette, studying it.

"It's the valley, Mr Benjamin. It's the shape of the valley, see. It's known for it hereabouts. It's an… an amp-lif-i-er, see. It takes the sound, and when the conditions are right it throws it all around, for miles."

I'd turned doubtfully to scan the fields.

"But he's literally miles away"

He'd nodded

"Known for it," he paused as if this explained everything. Then, a little more softly,

"Things carry round here, Mr Benjamin, especially on still days like this. You'll find that. Echo Valley right?"

Something had struck me as odd about this last remark, but I hadn't been able to place it.

"Echo Valley isn't its real name though is it, Mr Jones? It's called P-"

"Ahh," he'd interrupted and leaned forward conspiratorially. "But it'll do now, won't it? You know why now you've heard the bells and I've explained, eh?"

I'd paid him for the wood and watched the old truck drive away. As its drub faded, the sound of the bells had come again. I'd nodded slowly to myself.

'Sound carries round here,' he'd said. No. Wrong. That wasn't quite what he'd said.

*****

The light has almost gone now and the beer is finished. I deliberate about the next. It's easy to sit here and drink but I should be writing. The deadline is rolling up the road towards me, soon it will knock on the door. I stand, intending to at least visit the office, when I hear the first notes. It's a violin, and there's something else; a quick peal of laughter. I turn to the dark valley and see the lights; it's a small cluster about a mile away and I identify its source immediately. There's a house there, I first saw it in my early days in the valley. It sits about a mile away directly opposite. Through binoculars I'd picked out its gables and eaves showing above the stand of trees that sought to conceal it. I never wondered who lived there, only assuming that someone did, and also assuming that our lives would never intersect as there were no visible paths or easy route between us. I wondered now though – why hadn't I heard them before? Maybe this is the first time in all these months that conditions have been right. No, that doesn't explain the lights. Maybe they've just moved in.

Maybe it's a party. Welcome folks. Welcome to our new house in the valley. Oh I see you've brought a violin. Come in and have a drink, make a noise, it's ok we have no neighbours. Mind you, sound carries here.

As I watch another light goes on and blinks out again. Snatches of animated conversation come and go and the violin picks up pace. It's jazz, lively party jazz, old jazz. My head starts to nod to the beat and then I stop, distracted. I feel the deadline move closer with every passing moment. I feel my isolation, and most of all I feel heavy, alone in my world of no-Jane. I go to bed, and the last thing I hear before sleep comes is a long slow note on the violin followed by a round of distant applause.

*****

The next morning brings a crystal blue sky and the first frost of the year. A shallow mist hides the stream that runs through the valley. I scramble some eggs and carry my plate to the porch, looking across to the house again. I realise I can see it now without binoculars as the leaves on the intervening trees have all but gone. It's larger than mine and possibly stone built instead of brick, but because of the distance further detail eludes me.

Two hours of meaningful writing make me feel better. Then I reach for the telephone.

"Hello?" Mrs Jones' accent is broader than that of her husband and she answers the call hesitantly as if the phone itself is an object of suspicion.

"Mrs Jones? It's Nigel Benjamin. Is your husband there?"

"From up the valley." It's a statement rather than a question. She's telling me where I live as if to reconcile something before we can continue.

"Er, yes. From up the valley. Is he there?"

She hesitates, then, "Just wait now."

I wait for a full minute.

"Good morning, Mr Benjamin. Is it the wood again? Are you out?"

How does he know what I want?

"Yes. Yes it is actually. I'm using more now it's getting colder." I laugh. "How did you know?"

"Oh you know, it's been a while since your last lot and I figured you'd call soon."

Does he keep things like that in his head? Does he really? Or does he just pick up on my need for firewood from the air itself? Maybe he heard me move the last of the logs this morning. Sounds carry here after all.

"Are you in this afternoon, Mr Benjamin? I'll drive a load over."

"Yes I am. I'm in all day. I have to write."

There is a pause.

"You have to write, eh?" His tone is loaded, very subtly, but loaded. City boy has to write. City boy calls it work and it earns him bags of gold, enough for a fancy car. Well it's not work city boy. Farming is work. Moving sheep and managing the forest so you can have your firewood; that's work. Getting out of bed before dawn to repair the fencing and ripping your hands on barbed wire. Digging sheep out

70

of the snow while the ice whips your cheeks, that's work, boy.

"Yes. Write. I have a deadline." I say, making it worse. I don't care. You want to swap Jones? Maybe I'll come and move some sheep around and you can come into my world of heavy, my sad world of no-Jane.

"Well," he says. "You write then. I've a tractor to fix and then I'll load up and come over."

*****

When the wood is stowed, Jones surprisingly accepts my offer of a cup of tea and we sit together on the porch smoking. A little heat has crept into the day and the layer of mist is long gone. I gesture across the valley with my cup.

"I heard that lot last night." It's intentionally casual. He frowns. I gesture again.

"That house behind the trees. I've never heard them before. Maybe someone just moved in?"

He turns his head to where I indicate, pauses and then nods slowly without a word.

"Did you hear them?" I continue, "I mean, at the farm? It sounded like a party, maybe a house warming, eh?"

He turns to me and shrugs.

"No, boy, not a thing. Mind, I'm further away than you, see."

"I know but I thought you might have because… well… sound carries here right?"

He takes a large gulp of tea, seemingly keen to finish.

71

"Have you ever been up there, Mr Jones? How do you access that place? I guess it must have its own track from the Ludlow Road."

He turns his gaze back out over the valley, but he looks distracted now.

"No, boy, never been there. I never had the need, see."

Suddenly there's a shout from somewhere followed by a peal of laughter, a girl's voice. Then comes a sound of breaking twigs and branches from afar, as if people are running through trees. Jones and I stare across to the house. There's a flash of colour through the far trees, and for a moment I make out someone in a red coat. Other figures are dimly visible and they are in pursuit. I get a sense, not of threat, but of fun. Two words ring out followed by more laughter. It has the same distinct quality it had last night. Its clarity belies its distance. A trick of the valley I'm sure.

"Got you!"

Jones stands quickly and fastens his old jacket, ignoring our unknown neighbours. He offers me his cup.

"Thank you, Mr Benjamin. I have to get back now, the tractor won't fix itself."

I get up. His mood has changed very quickly.

"Er, ok. Well, thanks for the wood. That'll keep me going until Christmas I hope."

He grunts and walks towards his truck. I shout after him.

"I guess I was right, eh?"

"Eh?"

"It's a weekend party, someone has moved in."

He doesn't even glance back.

"Couldn't say."

I watch him go and then wander back to the porch. Whoever was in the trees has gone now and all is quiet. The shadows are lengthening and the temperature has dropped somewhat. It's time to write some more, time to get busy before the weight of the deadline and the sadness of no-Jane come calling.

*****

I didn't write though, did I? I sat for hours in the silent darkness and absorbed it. There was no music or merry laughter. It must have been a short weekend for our neighbours. Eventually sleep came, in the chair instead of the bed, and I dreamed of Jane. She sat with me on the rough porch and we joked about Jones. We ate sandwiches and drank beer and made plans. She seemed to know the house, which even in the dream struck me as odd.

I awake stiff and cold with a single notion in my head, so I shower and dress preparing to indulge it. I scan the valley as before with the binoculars, but this time with a purpose. After a minute or so I think I've got it – a route across to the other house through clear fields and fording the narrowest part of the stream.

By ten a.m. I'm striding out with the binoculars over my shoulder and an aluminium walking stick I'd bought way back when. The sun is pale and the day cold and still, but it's a pleasure to be out, and for a while the heaviness lifts a little. I have to move south east for a while to reach my chosen crossing place and I lose sight of the house behind the trees. I'm trying to work out what to say when I eventually reach it, what to say to them.

'Hi, I'm your neighbour from over yonder, how are you doing? Got any of that fine champagne left? Give us a tune, cheer me up. I'm a bit sad you see, a bit heavy. Why have I come here? I really don't know.'

There's a sharp sound from the bracken about fifty yards to my left and I freeze. A flash of russet as a large fox breaks cover and immediately spies me. It stops in an instant and holds statue still, meeting my gaze and poised for flight. Something floods in, something massive and every sense is engaged.

'Big threat. Slow threat. Not near. Watch.' The thoughts are not mine but are in my head. There's liquid metal in my mouth and I know it's the remnants of blood. I feel light and quick and full and frightened. My hands and knees are wet and I realise I'm on all fours on the grass. I can see myself there, but not though my eyes, and the colours are wrong.

Then it leaves and the fox is gone, back to the cover of bracken and bush.

I regain my feet and stand breathing heavily for a full five minutes trying to rationalise what's happened, but I can't. It's the beer and near sleepless night. It's the depression, the heavy. Or it's not. Eventually and irrationally the pull of the house reasserts itself.

By 11.30 I'm pulling myself up through the stand of pines that surround the house and its grounds. I drag my feet free of some brambles and there it is, tall and grey, gables and eaves, doors and windows. Broken. Deserted. Derelict. Devoid of life.

The front door is off one hinge and doesn't resist. I wander the rooms kicking shards of broken glass and fallen plaster. There's been no party here. Not this week or this year. Not for a long time. The rooms are big and tall and the peeling wallpaper – left to the elements for years I'd say – is colourful and thick. The rooms are almost completely empty, but lying on its side in a large drawing room that overlooks the valley, is a music stand, bent and rusting. There's a single sheet of paper face down next to it covered in plaster dust. I crouch and gingerly pick it up.

It's sheet music. Cole Porter, *Anything Goes*. It figures.

I don't know how long I've sat here now on the dirty floor, but the light is starting to fade. There are memories here but they're not mine. They're all around, as elusive as smoke but they somehow thicken the air. It's getting very cold now and at last I'm giving a thought to getting back across the valley when I hear laughter, a woman's laughter. It's a gay, easy sound, free of care and heavy. There's a pause and it comes again, followed by a man's voice, answering and somehow familiar.

I think I know now. I think I've got it. I rise and climb the grand staircase I'd found on my earlier tour. I move to the bedroom overlooking the trees and the valley and I stand by the broken window peering through the cold dusk. There are lights across the valley in the house opposite, my house. I briefly catch an impression of movement in an upper room and the man's voice again, my voice. Jane answers, calling from the porch, I think, and then she laughs again. Distant but clear.

It's a trick of the valley you see, a kind of amplification I believe. There's memory and feeling and hope and things that have been, but also things that might have been. Jones knows this and the fox knows this and now I know it too.

Things carry here.

BABY PLEASE DON'T GO

"Baby please don't go, down to New Orleans
You know I love you so, baby please don't go."
Big Joe Williams 1935.

I'm not the first guy to lose a girl and I won't be the last. Admittedly this all came on a little more quickly than previous rejections, but it still hurts like sharp ice. Once it's started to go it's never the same again, and you would be a foolish man to try and hang on. Most times she's turned for a reason, and whether it's something lacking between you, or the trembling allure of some new potential beau, when the magic has gone, it's gone.

You generally become, in spite of yourself, some cringing needy sap, all damaged pride and outrage. An ego fixated loser who can't allow the possibility that any girl could find a better alternative – a better use of her years on earth.

I don't feel that now however, this is different, and I'm going to put up a fight.

What is love anyhow? I heard a definition once that I liked. If you really love someone – it went – you will want the best for them, even if that means letting them go and leave you behind. Real love centres on the object of affection and not your relationship to it/her.

Well stuff that. All love is selfish. When we cry at a

77

funeral or bemoan the loss of a family member or friend, it's naïve to think we are mourning them. Indeed, we are simply crying for ourselves and the effect their loss will have on us, and the change it will make to our selfish life.

Yes, I'm going to fight this time. You're not Sarah Frazer, wooed by Jim Harris and then apparently by most of the sixth form. You're not Lisa with the crooked smile and suntan, who wandered down the beach one day and came back with a guilty look. You're not Emily, married to the American before our bloody bed was cold.

No, this is different. Besides, I have to make a supreme effort. It seems to be expected of me. I'll look foolish if I don't, stupid even.

The fact is that I really, really love you my girl. I never realised it properly until now, when the threat of life without you is looming large. I do need you to be happy, without me or not. But you know? It may as well be with me. It seems that all our time over the last five months has just condensed in my head.

You're beautiful you're arrogant you're a bit vain you're generous you're daring you're scared sometimes you're forgetful you're always honest you said you loved me you said it again and again…

"Don't leave me, girl!"

Yep, I screamed it. The mumbling crowd fall to silence and I continue to compress. Thirty down, two breaths. Again. Thirty down, two breaths.

"COME ON, BREATHE!"

I'm dragged off by the orange suits, the arbiters of your best chance now. The pavement is cold through my jeans and my shoulders ache from the efforts of the last five minutes. Someone places two hands on my shoulder and whispers in close.

"They've got her now, son. You did well."

I shake them off. C'mon you lovely warm cold selfish bitch, put up a fight.

Baby please don't go.

DEAD CELEBRITY

My great grandfather, according to a somewhat unreliable family history, used to work the rigging on the last of the tall ships out of Liverpool. I have few memories of him now, and the ones I do have are almost certainly skewed by the images in old photograph albums. I think I falsely remember the young man staring with sepia and sodium light eyes, a glass of beer raised to the world, instead of the broken old fellow at whose knee I would sit on winter Fridays. I do recall the stories however, clear as day. They would be tales of the sea or of the countryside, tales of his youth, of hard work with hands already roughened by salt and grime and of a world where things were better – or at least a world where things ended better. They were shot through with colour and humour, and in hindsight, I'm sure, more than a little fiction. Occasionally, until the telling was stopped by my mother or father, they would be stories of khaki, mud and metal – of noise and flame and friends lost.

Sometimes they would be complete in one telling, and sometimes, as my head drooped with the heat of the fire and the exertions of a long day, the words would slow, winding down, and he would say:

"Ah well. We'll find the end of this one hanging on the back of tomorrow's door".

You see, I want to tell you what I'm seeing now, right in front of me. I want to tell you the impossibility of it, what it means and how the night has frozen in its progress towards day. I want to tell you how the blood has pooled in my feet and the how the hair has risen, stiff and cold on my neck. I want to tell you that the world is not how you think it is. No, not at all my friend.

Ever seen a ghost? I'm not sure that I have – even now. But I've seen this, and I'm going to tell you about it in a while. First there has to be some context though, some reason behind the unreason. I have to tell you all about her, and about obsession. The end of the story I'll have to leave for a while, we'll arrive there soon enough, but for now it's hanging on the back of tomorrow's door…

★★★★★

Arabella Raymon had risen to fame quickly as the zeitgeist seems to dictate these days. It seemed that she came from nowhere. There were a few short months as the lesser known third member of a middling girl band. Then there was a PR guru who saw a rare talent before anybody else did, and seized the moment with a shark's instinct – smelling contractual weakness and gold.

Arabella moved at first in my peripheral awareness, her progress detailed in the celebrity adjuncts of more serious news programmes. She was clearly beautiful, and as her fame grew it seemed her grooming and poise sharpened. She perfected a look to camera, a forehead-lowered-slightly-surprised-by-the-attention flash that would have been genuinely endearing if it wasn't obviously manufactured. She became meat for the cameras and heavy snacking for the tabloids. On the release of her first album the frenzy suddenly took hold. Everyone knew her name, and her image fired the aspirations of a million sink estate schoolgirls and the wet dreams of a similar number of teenage boys.

I didn't take much of an interest for quite some time. Of course I didn't. I was in my late forties and married with a son. The shelves in my office were a testament to my age and musical heritage. *Genesis* albums shared the dust with *Camel* and *Uriah Heep*. Photograph albums detailed the stoned weekends of yesteryear, red eyed with a retard grin at various festivals, wearing various t-shirts and various girlfriends. There was no reason at all for me to take any more than a passing interest in the career or personal life of someone whose target audience was my son's age.

I say again. The last thing on my mind was taking an interest in this girl's life.

But of course I did, and even now, at this moment, looking at… this, I'd do anything to wind back the clock, to turn back time, summon any cliché in fact, and just be out of this room…

First, I suppose, there was the voice and music. Desert Island Discs had faded to Woman's Hour on the day I first heard her speak. It was as I pushed the Volkswagen through the weather past Manchester. Normally I would have switched over at this point and never heard it or her. But the driving rain and erratic progress of an eastern European HGV kept my mind from the radio. When it returned she was talking, introducing the title track from her first album. My hand reached for the tuner and then stopped. There are some women's voices that come from a harsh place, some that are just soft, and some that ride joyfully on moving breath as they sing to you. Arabella's was the latter, and it occurred then that this was the first time I'd heard her talk. She spouted none of the airhead youth speak that passes for conversation with so many of her age and ilk. She spoke thoughtfully and humbly about her impending fame, and I found myself drawn in by the rhythm and tone of her voice. It seemed that there was more to what she was saying than simply the words. There was an undercurrent, a subtext, an embedded message that – yes, I know how this will sound – spoke to me personally.

The words became music, a simple song backed by a single acoustic and tom toms. It overpowered the note of the engine and the rain, not by its volume but by its... presence. There were undercurrents here too, images of soft warm hills and grass, yellow sunlight, and somehow, unnervingly, right at the back of the mix, surely only in my imagination, screaming.

I listened to the song and the rest of the interview, and then pulled into the next services for a coffee. I was exhausted, elated, and deeply puzzled.

*****

Two weeks later, Marianne found the album in my car. We were on our way to Tom's recital at the school, and the CD was on the passenger seat as she got in.

"What's this, love?"

Marianne and I share a taste and enthusiasm for music, always have done. I turned to her a little sheepishly. By then I'd made several visits to Arabella's website and even bought a couple of celebrity magazines. I guess I was already a clandestine fan.

"It's a CD, isn't it?"

"Is it Tom's?"

"No, it's mine." There, not a secret any more. Her eyes narrowed, not with suspicion – yet – but with genuine curiosity.

"Yours? Arabella fucking Raymon? You're kidding right?"

I put the car into gear and moved off.

"No. It's good. I heard a couple of tracks on the radio. You should listen to some."

"Babe, this girl doesn't have any pubic hair yet. I would have been surprised if it was Tom's, let alone yours."

I laughed and she did too.

"Go on, put it on. Go on".

She did, and we listened as we drove. As always the music spoke to me, as always the images came, and, as of more recently, the scent came too. Just a hint of wildflowers and a dense perfume lurked about the cabin, and I guess I understood at some level right then that Marianne would not smell it or even hear the music in the way that I could. There was another smell too, so slight as to be almost undetectable, but it wrinkled my nostrils as I listened. It was earth. Wet earth. Old earth. It was there and then it wasn't.

"Well?"

I stopped in the school car park and ejected the CD. Marianne tilted her head.

"Well, I've got to say it's a bit more mature than I was expecting, but I'm still amazed it does anything for you."

She sat back and put a hand on my arm.

"Christ. You prat. It's a joke, isn't it? I fell for it, didn't I?"

I frowned, feeling a curious outrage.

"Hey no! I really like it. Maybe we're all a little too rigid in our tastes, eh? C'mon give it a chance."

"I just did my love, and it's ok, just ok alright? For God's sake don't let Tom know you've bought this, you know how kids are about their dad trying to appear 'trendy'? He'll take an overdose."

I was riled now. There might have been some embarrassment there as well, a kind of 'caught out' guilt, but the irritation won.

"Look, just back off, Marianne. I like this music, ok? This girl is different, she's special…"

I knew straight away I'd crossed a line. I had spoken with too much sincerity to pass it off as a joke now. Marianne's expression changed. It wasn't worry yet – though I would see that soon enough – it was… discomfort. She leaned back, frowning. I'm sure it was unconscious, but definitely symbolic of trying to put a little distance between us, trying to avoid association by proximity.

She opened the door and the night blew in.

"Anyway, Tom's playing in a minute. Let's go and hear some real bloody music shall we?"

★★★★★

After that I kept my new enthusiasm to myself. With every tabloid magazine that I read over a sandwich at lunchtime, and all the hours on my laptop examining the minutiae of Arabella's life, somewhere at the back of my mind I knew that Marianne was right. It was strange, somehow a little dirty, for a man of my years and situation to be this fixated. However, my fascination was consuming, and that overrode all the protocols that would normally have stopped me.

I tried to hear the real girl behind every facile quote, tried to imagine her in poses and situations not revealed in the paparazzi pictures, eating lunch, brushing her teeth, kissing. The strangest thing was that none of this was overtly sexual. True, some part of me wanted her, but she had a boyfriend – a well-documented relationship – and I didn't feel a tinge of jealousy, in fact I wished them well. She was photographed dancing in nightclubs and I didn't for one moment wish that it was me grinding and twisting the night away with her.

No. What I felt was more basic. It was like a need to protect, to gain knowledge. It was, in hindsight, a hunger, and it was borne of the fact that at some deep level, somehow, I knew she would need me someday, that I might be chosen.

I think I crossed a line the first time that I lied to Marianne.

"It was joke, alright? I didn't send for it." I faced Marianne across the kitchen table. It was Saturday morning and she had borrowed my car to go to her classes. She had found – looked for? – the envelope in the glove box. Now it lay, thrown down, on the table between us. She held up the letter she had removed and read from it, her voice pitched high.

'Paul,

You lovely person. I want to thank you so much for joining the club, I'm sorry that this couldn't be a personal letter but I'm sure you understand how many of you there are! I'll be sure and send you details of all my forthcoming releases and tour dates. I'm so grateful you've chosen to take an interest in me and what's going on in my life. I couldn't have reached where I am without you and thousands like you, so big hugs and kisses until we meet. Maybe I'll see you at the O2 in June? You can get a massive discount if you quote the fan number enclosed. In the meantime, wear your Big A badge with pride!

Love,

A.xxx'

Marianne had reached inside the envelope and found the badge. She held it up for me to see. I'd already seen it, again and again. There was a picture of Arabella winking cheekily above the Big A logo that had become her brand. She waited for me to speak.

"James sent for it. They found the CD in the car and gave me the same grief you did. They sent my details, ok?"

It was all I had. The lie would stop there.

Marianne had shaken her head but I still couldn't read her.

"You know what I think, my love? I think you're a Big A. A big arsehole. If you let the guys at work find that CD then you're *just* a big arsehole. If you're lying to me and you actually are a member of this girl's fan club then

87

you're a huge arsehole, a universe spanning arsehole of cosmic proportions."

I know my wife, and in that moment I knew she believed me. It would be humour and sarcasm from now on and not, thank God, an awkwardness borne of the fact that her husband was genuinely strange. We had both laughed, maybe that was the last time we did. She flounced out of the kitchen en route to the shower, and I took the fan club badge from the table. Arabella Raymon looked at me through the one, non-winking eye. A strange thought came to me. It only takes one eye to wink, but you need to see the other eye open to know it's a wink – otherwise it's just one shut eye. The wink only has context alongside the open eye. Like Arabella and me.

And oh, that open eye. It fixed me as it did every time I had held up the badge. I knew that she was looking at me and me alone. I knew somehow that at the moment the picture had been taken she had been searching into the camera for me. There was something wild in that gaze, something old and something destined. There was something of trees and still deep water.

That eye wanted to pull me in. It wanted to fascinate and scare me. It did both.

★★★★★

As the weeks moved along I spent a lot of time on the internet. Searching, researching, and scribbling down every small detail of Arabella's life in my notebook. Thankfully Marianne had a lot of girlfriends and attended a lot of fitness classes. We'd always agreed that our independent interests had an important place in the marriage. She had book club, boxercise and white wine and I had my rowing, my photography and my mates. Or at least I did have. I had Arabella now.

I have no idea exactly when I moved from unhealthy interest to obsession, but I undoubtedly had. I think the tattoo was evidence of that. It was a small 'A' on the bottom of my foot. I'd seen the craze start on the internet. The fan sites detailed the queues of young girls at the parlours, waiting for their chance to register their small, permanent dedication to the Arabella Raymon phenomenon.

I'd finished work early one afternoon and sourced the most obscure studio I could find.

"You want what mate?"

He was a large man, sitting like a pierced and painted Buddha on the swivel chair in the back room.

"That's that Arabella what's 'er name, innit? You sure mate? I ain't done one of them. Why'd you want one of them?"

"I just do alright? It's… It's a joke. For a bet."

"Some fuckin' bet, mate. It don't rub off, y'know?" The studio-cum-office was shared by a diffident Goth girl who served as a receptionist. She shook her head and they shared a look.

"Whatever, mate, it's your money. Get on the chair. Is it on your arm?"

"No. The bottom of my foot."

They both stared at me for a few moments.

"This is really going to fucking hurt."

★★★★★

I'd limped to the car, trying to remember the last time that Marianne or Tom had seen the bottom of my foot. I'd just have to be careful, that's all. I'd driven home recklessly as Arabella was appearing on a chat show at ten o'clock and I'd not programmed the TV to record. Thankfully they were both out and I settled down with a beer and a sandwich as Arabella flounced into the studio to wild applause. She looked stunning in a shiny gold mini dress and the host stood to greet her with an air kiss. They talked the usual rubbish, or at least he did. Arabella's replies and input were as always sharp and witty. He was outclassed and knew it and soon he began to resort to sly quips about her private life in order to regain the upper hand. He alluded to rumours that Mr Rock Star Boyfriend had been seen about the town with someone else. I felt irked that my girl had to endure this and I put a hand out to touch her face.

When had I moved from the sofa to kneel in front of the screen?

Arabella, who had been staring down smoothing her dress, suddenly shot him a look that had the power and speed of a bullet. He sat back, no, recoiled on his sofa and dropped his notes. The audience were similarly stunned to silence. She hadn't said a word, but no one was in any doubt about her meaning. They may not have sensed the feral power and malice in the way that I did, or smelled the wave of cinders and loam and decay that rode on the stare she gave him. If they had they would have felt horror. I just felt desire.

Then the strangest thing happened. Arabella looked to camera, all traces of threat gone in an instant. She gave the sweetest smile and beckoned. I guess that somewhere in the monitor suite the producer had sensed a 'television' moment and screamed "Zoom!" to the bemused cameraman, for suddenly her face filled the screen.

"You know what?" she said to the watching millions (No, just to me). "I don't care about any of that. There's my special man out there waiting for me. He knows who he is and pretty soon we'll be together." She winked. "Won't we?"

She gave a small chuckle that was both sweet and cruel and the audience suddenly burst into spontaneous applause. I guess it was borne of relief more than anything else as they were given leave to banish the awkward tension of the last few seconds.

I felt a release of tension as well, and with just a tug of shame, pulled my sticky hand from the front of my jeans and laid it on the screen, looking at her beautiful face between my outstretched fingers.

Arabella stood and walked out of the studio, leaving the flustered host to splutter his excuses and make light of whole episode, and I knew in that moment that all of it had been about me. She'd had something to say and somehow she had reached down the airwaves and found me. I knew for sure now that she wanted me, that I was chosen.

There was a sudden scrape on the carpet as the living room door opened and Marianne entered clutching a bottle of wine with two of her friends in tow. Tom was there was well, they had picked him up from orchestra practice.

I turned my head and just stared at them. They became statues.

"Paul. What the hell?"

★★★★★

I'd been sleeping in James' spare room for some weeks. I guess it was inevitable after the television episode. There's not much to James apart from football and beer, so he had accepted my situation without analysis and had just done the decent bloke thing. Tom had called me a couple of times but I could feel his embarrassment over the line, we talked about sport and music and the like, but really he just wanted to get off and forget that he has a father who abuses himself in front of the TV. During our infrequent conversations, Marianne was frosty but realistic. She knew that we had stuff to sort out. I think there was still love there. I had plenty of love of course, trouble is, it was all for Arabella.

The first thing I'd done was to write to the fan club informing them of my change of address. Thank God they'd updated their records quickly, because yesterday I'd received notification that Arabella was expected to attend the premiere of a new film in Leicester Square next week. That was it then, I'd finally see her in the flesh. We'd have a... coming together, and everyone would see. She would have to search no more, for I would answer her call, and would be chosen.

I sighed and dropped the notification on my laptop. Chosen. What did that even mean?

*****

It was a lovely early summers evening in central London and I left the cab at a run. The square was cordoned off and I felt a small twinge of panic as I hadn't anticipated this many people. I held my camera steady as I jostled and squeezed through the masses, I had bought it just to appear a little less suspicious amongst the mostly teenage crowd. You know how it is, props serve us well – man walking alone in a field? Bit weird. Man walking alone in a field swinging a dog lead? No problem – All you weirdoes take note. I didn't want any photos of her, oh no. I wanted to touch and speak, as I was sure she did too. I've never been a rude or an impolite man, but I made quite a few enemies that evening en route to the roped off carpet. Thankfully not many people were old enough or big enough to make an issue of it. Eventually I secured a tenuous slot about halfway along the carpet amid a noisy gaggle of young flesh. There were already celebrities of varying degrees of fame and ability being shepherded past the mob. Each one was accompanied by security, and each one garnered a cheer appropriate to their credibility and perceived coolness. As the star of the film, a young American, schmoozed past accompanied by his favoured interviewer and a steady cam operator, my immediate neighbourhood erupted with piercing screams and I swear I could smell the hormones. I looked down the line, praying to God that I hadn't missed her. I craned forward, almost overbalancing and my camera had swung into the back of a teenage girl with pigtails. She spun round.

"Oi! What's your game?"

The look of annoyance had quickly changed however to one of confused recognition.

"Hey, you're Mr. Hannay. What are you doing here?" She had to shout to be heard.

Her name was Jemma and she was in Tom's music class. I had given her a lift home on a number of occasions. Shit.

"Jemma. Hi." I held up the camera. "I... I'm just getting some pictures for Tom. He... He couldn't come."

It sounded lame and her expression had changed to a frown. Luckily some other minor celebrity driftwood sashayed past at that moment and Jemma got distracted. I watched her and the gaggle of almost identically dressed teens as they held up their camera phones and brayed for a second of this nobody's attention. What the hell was I doing here? Tom didn't need any further embarrassment from me.

A second later and I knew why I was there.

To a cheer that almost shook the pavement, Arabella Raymon eased out a limo at the end of the line. I gasped and elbowed some kid out of the way to be next to the rope. Flanked by two minders and dressed to kill in a crop top and mini skirt, she began a poised and purposeful walk towards the entrance, ignoring everyone. They screamed, they pleaded and they reached, but no one could even get a cheeky wink... and I wanted so much more than that.

She was about twenty feet away when she slowed and began to scan the crowd. The brutes in the suits exchanged irritated glances, and one took her arm, continuing to walk. There was obviously a schedule. The man was about three times her weight and should have been able to move her like a feather, however he suddenly jerked backwards as if he had been trying to pull a tractor. Arabella stayed rooted to the spot, eyes running up and down my side of the line. I felt words form in my mouth.

"Arabella! Here!"

The ambient noise was such that I couldn't hear my own voice, but a moment later her head slowly turned. Our eyes met, and her face lit with an expression I can only describe as joy. I swear that my heart stopped. We held our gaze as she walked right up to me and stopped.

"Special man. There you are."

I thought for a moment that my concentration and focus was such that all the background noise was being blanked out. It wasn't, most of it had ceased. I turned away and regarded the people crowded around. Jemma and her friends were dumbstruck, gaping like fish, their phones held out in front like talismans.

"Look at me special man!" She was not to be denied. I slowly turned back and met her eyes. I can't describe properly what happened then, Arabella pulled with her mind and I felt myself empty. Information and will were sucked out in a moment. I was laid bare. I had never been so aroused or so scared.

"It'll be our time soon, Paul, our time to move on. I've been waiting so long." There were things behind those deep gorgeous eyes, old things, wet things, and I knew I would see them soon. She reached up and placed one hand behind my head, pulling me close. I was dimly aware of the minders stepping forward.

"Now listen, Paul."

She knew my name. I couldn't even think of how. There were too many questions, and I had to remember to breathe.

"You are mine now. I know you and all that you are. Soon you will know me."

I was pulled further into her wonderful, awful gaze, and I think that for a moment I saw more than I was meant to. I saw an almost desperate need, a longing that was both ancient and corrupt. It awoke something that broke like a wave and shook me. I was suddenly standing outside of myself looking down at a small sad man in a crowd of children. The last few months were revealed to me in a series of linear snapshots, a pathetic and inevitable fall from grace, an obsession in which I was complicit and an inexplicable hunger that I had satisfied without thought of the consequences. At the centre of it all was Marianne, duped and humiliated, and now, unless I could change the world somehow, lost to me. I knew then that I must try to make it all right, even though it was almost undoubtedly too late.

Arabella drew back and gave me that wink again, the one from the badge. I realised something then and the thought bought a new level of weird with it. She had never spoken. Her lips had never moved. I had simply understood.

Then she was gone, this time hooking both her arms into those of her minders and giggling her way towards the open doors.

"What the bloody hell? Do you know her Mr. Hannay?"

I looked down at Jemma. I could almost see the cogs in her head whirring with the social possibilities of her friend's father actually being a mate of Arabella Raymon. For no rational reason I slipped the camera from around my neck and thrust it into her hands.

"No. Not any more, Jemma."

I turned and began to push past the faces and the shoulders and the stares.

★★★★★

I was a passenger from that point onwards, driven by a powerful vehicle over which I had no control. I asked no questions and looked for no reasons.

There were two bars, or maybe three. I moved on every time my expression or intensity became suspicious. At two fifteen the following morning I took a taxi and gave my proper address. At five to three I stopped him at the end of the drive and pushed the gate open. I had no idea what I was going to say to Marianne or Tom, but I would ask for their forgiveness, their understanding.

The garden was washed by the full moon, and most of the lights were on inside. The front door was ajar, and as I moved inside the kitchen light went out. There was someone in there. That's where I would start.

★★★★★

We've arrived now, my friend, we're at the back of tomorrow's door. It's time to see what's hanging there.

The slatted blinds filter the sharp moonlight that streams into the kitchen. Everything is revealed in argent and black tiger stripes. Arabella sprawls on the central island amongst a silence so deep it hurts my ears. She is propped up on both hands and staring directly at me. I can see her chest heave in and out of black shadow with every quick, noiseless breath. The air in the room is cold and yet somehow thick, and my nose fills with the now familiar odour. Eau d'Arabella. Eau d'ancienne. Eau de mort. It seems I've forgotten how to breathe but I can move my eyes, so I tear them away push my gaze into the recesses of my kitchen. There are things I must see, things that must be there. Things that wait for my attention, their detail stretched in a colourless greyscale from silver to deepest black.

Blackest of all is the blood that has pooled from poor Marianne's neck and now wets my shoes. She lies twisted and flattened like road kill on the kitchen floor. There appears to be gap, a wide tear, a rent at the point her neck has snapped, and it is curiously spanned by her gold necklace which is still intact and glowing in the moonlight.

"She didn't love you, Paul. I love you."

It's not a voice; its words are formed of moving breath. It draws me back to regard the mouth that issues them. The full gloss of those gorgeous lips and permanent kiss shape of the diva's mouth has gone. There's a round hole where they used to be and it's edges are rolled out and fluted like a cartoon fish. They vibrate with the air that forms her words and I get an impression of concentric rows of needle teeth set in the wet behind them.

"I chose you, Paul. I chose you long ago. You've always been mine."

I don't react because I can't. I don't feel horror because what I do feel goes beyond that and doesn't have a name. There's a mass of images pushing into my head, they're trying to replace something and each small impression, each vignette has its own smell, some familiar, some not. There are those hot hills again, tall trees – cypress? – and there's a man who grunts as he hefts a sword. I'm almost sick at the stench of dead earth. The man is naked and I watch as he falls on the blade. His blood is red, not black. He dies with a profound shudder and one word:

'Lamia.'

Then there are children naked in a shaded pool. They're splashing and screeching and teasing each other, patting lily pads like drums. It's hot and humid but the water is cool. I know this. The reeds and the lilies should smell strong with high summer and healthy stagnation but they don't. They smell of what shares their pool. There's a black woman at the water's edge, maybe a slave, and I know she is responsible for the children. I can see her eyes become saucers now and can hear her scream. A child goes down, pulled to the depths in an instant by some invisible agent. There's not even a splash.

And all of this is Arabella. This is what she is and has been.

Oh my sweet. My Big A. You've been with us for so long, haven't you?

I shake my head and her history briefly disappears. I look down at the floor again. I look at what used to be my boy, Tom, just visible at the side of the kitchen island. His face is frozen in mid scream, a rictus grin. There's a mess around him that used to be him. He's not what he was.

I'm breathing again now, slow and deep. Some part of me is

pulled towards what Arabella is trying to suppress. I know it's my last chance to feel anything before it goes forever and so I must give it some attention. She's pulling my memories out of me. I look again at Marianne and encounter a bluster of images, each one stabbing me like a tiny knife. Smiles and shared laughter, a day by the sea, hard sex, soft sex, an argument and a truce, a Christmas tree falling down and a tear on her cheek. This is all I was and nothing of what I will be.

The memories pop like bubble wrap and go forever. Arabella has let me have them one last time and now she has taken them, for I have indeed been chosen. She lets me know I'm a special man, I always was. There have been others throughout the ages, all men, human anchors that allow her to exist here in whatever guise she chooses. Now she is Arabella, but before that she was Claudia and before that Myrthia and before that a woman from a time where they did not give names. She chooses her man, anchors to him and it keeps her stable in this world.

Then she can feed. Feed on fame and flesh. For that is all there is.

She moves for me now and rears up as I take a step to meet her. Her hair and eyes are what they were and I feel a fierce desire as a lock falls over one eye and she gives me that look again. That Big A tease. She is still wearing the short dress from the red carpet, but what emerges from the hem has changed. The moonlight doesn't allow a full view, but an impression is enough – too much. That sickly, pale, moist slug tail flexes as she rises up. I can taste earth, taste everything that has gone before.

Just a slow kiss now, just what I've wanted for a long time, and a soft embrace.

ETIQUETTE

A dark autumn wind wipes the rain across the restaurant windows and seizes the coat tails of those who stand in the queue, threatening to carry them far and wide to less popular haunts. Yet they stand firm, determined and patient. This is the place to eat. They do things properly here.

Inside, amidst the fashionable gloom and candlelight, flutes chink and fine cutlery scrapes bone china as the patrons consume. There is conversation, but it is discreet. It carries not the self-conscious hush of embarrassment or the strut of indifference. A glass is emptied and the sommelier weaves across the room without fuss or urgency to refill it. A napkin is dropped, and within seconds is scooped from the floor and a clean one placed upon grateful knees. They do things properly here.

Table four, neither the best nor the worst in the house, entertains Jerome and Matilda. It's a first date. He is tall, casual and perfectly at home. She is shorter, and less so. He takes a sip of wine and leans back.

"So, the soup?"

She shrugs and gives a short smile.

"Yeah, I ordered the soup. I always have the soup. I get too full otherwise."

"Oh yeah, too full for what?"

Her smile thins. She still likes him, though not quite as much as a moment ago.

"For the steak."

He holds up his hands and rolls his eyes.

"Sorry, that was a rubbish thing to say."

"Yeah. Rubbish."

There is a moment's silence, and then they laugh. The tension floats away. Most of it.

He holds his glass and her eyes.

"To you, Matilda. Thanks for coming."

She looks to her glass uncertainly and screws her nose.

"Can I drink to myself? I'm not sure I can. Is it done? Is it etiquette?"

He shrugs.

"I dunno. Is it important?"

She's mischievous now.

"Yes. Etiquette is important. My dad was always strict about that."

"Was he? But I can't see him in here."

"No, you wouldn't, he's in heaven."

"Oh. Is he?"

The tension is back. Then she raises her glass and breaks a killer smile.

"No stupid. But he is dead. Here's to me?"

He joins her in the toast.

"Well. I guess it's ok then. Nothing bad has happened."

As their glasses touch the waiter appears wearing a professional smile. They part and regard what he carries.

"Soup for the lady?"

It's a shallow white bowl.

"And oysters for sir."

It's placed with a flourish.

"Enjoy."

They begin their meal. Each slightly aware of the lack of wisdom they have shown in their choices. Not first date food, one potentially messy, one potentially noisy. There's always the chance that they will betray themselves with a careless move, an embarrassing slurp. Therefore they eat carefully and take their time, punctuating the *hors d'ouvres* with small conversation.

"So, what other points of etiquette did your dad insist upon?"

"Well, he was a snob, although I can't think why. We were quite poor and it's not as if we ever came to a place like this."

A wave of cold air circles the room as the next lucky couple are admitted to a polite greeting and the taking of coats.

"He was particularly hot on soup."

"Ah, we're back to soup."

"Indeed we are. You always dip your spoon away from you while tipping the bowl towards yourself."

He nods.

"That's right. You do. One does, but what about custard for example?"

"Custard?" A sly smile. "I never order custard to start."

"Of course, but custard is a liquid, just like soup. If you had bowl of custard in front of you now instead of that fine mock-turtle, how would you eat it?"

"I would scoop the spoon towards me."

"Why?"

"Because it feels natural."

"And yet with soup it's always away from you. Is that unnatural?"

She considers.

"Yes actually it is. But soup is soup and custard is custard."

She leans forward conspiratorially.

"It's the law. It's etiquette."

He dabs his mouth and discards another shell.

"How unnatural? If I were to ask you to eat your soup by scooping it custard fashion with your spoon, how bad would that feel? How wrong on a scale of one to ten?"

She sits back, processing.

"D'you know? About eight or nine. I would hate to do it. I guess it became ingrained at a very early age and now… well… ugh. It would feel so wrong!"

"Illegal?"

"Not illegal, stupid, just very wrong."

"And… how about… ooh let's say broth?"

"Broth?"

"Yes. Is broth a soup? It's thicker and has large bits in it. Almost a stew one might say. How would you eat that?"

"Oh please, let's not drill down that much."

Nevertheless she considers it.

"Well I'd… I'd definitely scoop away. It's a soup, or at least it's in the soup section on the supermarket shelves."

They share a genuine laugh, the first. Both hands being occupied with the oyster shell and napkin, he juts his chin and raises his eyebrows.

"Go on, just one mouthful."

"What?"

"Just one small mouthful of that lovely expensive soup, scooped towards you. Go on, girl."

"No, get lost. Eat your own food and leave me alone."

"Go on. What would happen?"

"I've said what. I would feel wrong, as if I'd... I dunno... held a cigarette between my third finger and little finger, as though I'd started a loud phone conversation in a library. It's just not done. It's wrong..." She giggles. "... As if some fundamental law of the universe had been broken."

"'Just not done', maybe we're getting somewhere. So go on, just one mouthful? I dare you. We'll come back to the cigarette thing."

"Bugger off."

Her tone is still light but there is more irritation. He's playing a daft game, messing with her.

"Are you scared a waiter may see? Or... someone else?"

"I don't care about that, besides they've got too much class and respect here to say anything. Unless you started to break wind loudly and repeatedly I guess."

"Trust me I won't. That's second date stuff."

"Ahh, then you plan to ask me out again?"

He looks thoughtful, and then deadly serious.

"Well, that depends. I reckon you have maybe three spoonfuls of soup left. If you scoop one of them towards you then it's a weekend at Claridges."

There are long seconds of silence now as they hold

each other's eyes. The restaurant door is opened once more and another wet couple express gratitude at their change of circumstances.

"You're not kidding, are you?"

"Nope. Just one spoonful."

"Separate beds?"

"Three thousand quid a night, are you kidding?"

"Ha!" And then, "Ok."

She takes a deep breath and glances to the left and right. The spoon hovers over the far edge of the bowl for a moment and is then scooped towards her, trawling soup. Her head dips to meet it and the contents are sucked and devoured.

"There. Book it."

The confident, easy smile spreads once more across his face, but it is altogether more reptilian now, as is his skin that glistens with the scales that have surfaced upon it. His lips part, a forked tongue darting out to sniff the air. As her eyes widen, the floor shakes, and from somewhere far below there comes a bass rumble, felt in the stomach and at the lower range of hearing. All eyes in the place are upon her, staff and customers with knowing smiles. Instantly the floor beneath her splits and smoky rays of crimson light distort her features from below. Up from the rent slide clawed hands, green with slime and foul earth. The fingernails upon them are impossibly long and sharp, and before she can react, one has entered her right ear and pushed through her head, snapping and slurping through its contents. As it emerges from the other side it crooks and wraps around her hair. Both she and her chair are snatched downwards and in a moment nothing of her remains.

As quickly as it opened, the rent closes and the remaining few cloying strands of sulphur smoke drift away.

Jeromiapha summons a waiter with a delicate flick of his forked tounge. He is a respected customer of long standing, an ancient Sumerian etiquette demon long consigned to this realm to police and punish small transgressions of cosmic law. He asks quietly, in a language that died a thousand years before the fall of Babylon, for his plate to be removed. The waiter performs this small task discreetly and with unforced politeness.

They do things properly here.

SHY

I've been watching you for some time. I've been waiting for my moment, that rare moment, that instant when all the little uncertainties and myriad variables line up just right. That sweet second when the universe stills its confusion and slows its giddy chaos just long enough so that one can act quickly and with clarity.

I've noticed that you have a routine. That's no surprise. We're all creatures of habit they say. I've got to hand it to you though, you sashay and bounce through your day with a refreshing spirit. As an observer of people I know this. I've watched a few, shoulders down, bad posture, loaded up with their troubles. You've got a spring to your step whatever the weather, rain or shine. You breeze down the city street each morning in one of your skirt suits or, of course, jeans on Fridays, and your manner says, 'I own the day!'

'Good morning, doughnut man!'

'Hi there girl coming the other way who I seem to know well enough to pass the time of day with but not stop for a real chat.'

'Thanks for the newspaper, newspaper guy! My hair? Well thank you!'

All these people and more move in and around your orbit and I'm sure they are better off for the brief experience, a brief flash of light to carry with them through the day. Lucky you. Bright you. Pretty girl.

Of course it's different for me. I have to know you better than that. I have to know you real well. That's why my moment is so important.

Of course I've been close to you. It's all part of the plan, the preparation. Three days ago you left your house in a hurry and forgot your laptop. I'd just pulled away from the kerb to follow your car when guess what? You braked just in front of me with no warning, and ran back to the house. I think I'd have shouted or at least flipped you the finger, if you hadn't have been you. At least I merited a quick, waved apology and flash of that eyebrow sloping frowny smile you own. Of course I had to drive away then.

Then there was the coffee shop. From where I stood one back in the queue I could just detect fresh coconut. What is that? Shampoo? Body oil? The latter I think. I particularly liked your blouse that day – you do co-ordinate well, you know.

Of course I'm seldom that close. You can't smell through glass, and I wanted to get a scent and a sense of the real you before I make my move. Call me shy if you like, I have to plan my moment from afar. I've always been awkward with girls, right from school. The army didn't help – months and months without a sniff of 'how'd ya do', and then they chuck you some leave and you're positively encouraged to pay for it. Jesus, it's no wonder your social skills suffer.

You however, sweetheart, are going to be nothing but good for me. There's flights and a room already booked.

It's a beautiful place on the Italian lakes. It's rumoured that Byron stayed there. Very expensive. Very exclusive. I just know you're worth it. Someone thinks so anyhow. It's all because of you.

No, you can't smell through glass, nor can you hear at this distance. From the tenth floor the street sounds are muted, even the traffic. It gives a guy a chance to concentrate. Here you come with your morning swagger. Three breaths now and we're consummated. Steady steps as always. Crosshairs razor sharp and suddenly your head fills the glass. Auburn hair flicking in the breeze. Seven miles an hour from the south.

Third breath.

You know what? I think I'm falling in love with you.

Squeeze.

THE AIR RACE

The salt wind lifted the girl's hair as she made her way carelessly over the grassy hilltop on the way back to town. Her eyes were raised to the blue above and the high cold clouds. Now and then she would swing her school bag in wide circles and let her body follow it round, pivoting, letting its weight propel her. Then she would stop, the sky continuing to turn, making her sway until both ears balanced once more. There was no path to follow, just an expanse of short tough grass broken by sprays of wild flowers, and more rarely by a rising lark against high cumulus. It was these, along with other small distractions that pulled for her attention as she walked and dreamed, as always, of the sky.

Presently the hill crested and the sky became the sea, the first roofs and towers of the town showing orange and white against it. She stopped and watched a steamboat enter the harbour. Silent at this distance and reduced to a silhouette by the sun on the water, it slowed as it approached and manoeuvred around a smaller craft, coming gently to rest against the harbour wall. Its silhouette resolved into colour and she saw people lining the rail, three or four deep, waving. Their waves were received and returned by those on the quay who had been waiting for the boat. Men made the ropes fast and the

111

boat's horn gave one deep, rude note as disembarkation began. The girl shaded her eyes and tried to pick out individuals in the crowd, but their summer colours and sunhats blended into one, blurred with the heat and distance.

The girl hugged her school bag to her chest and felt a small excitement. The crowds were gathering for the air race, and her small town, so long on the margins, was to be the focus, if only for a couple of weeks, of the finest attention.

"Semi-finals, eh?" her father had announced one evening, as fish fried on the veranda and her mother fussed over the fire, refusing all help and leaving the girls to chase the early fireflies or watch the sunset from the low wall over the sea. He had folded the news sheet.

"That's a coup to be sure. Five towns in the running and it goes to us. Where will they mark the course, eh girls?"

Catherine, who had appeared disinterested, immediately replied

"The heath of course! Up high. On the grasslands by the cliffs."

"No," this was Della, "the sand. We are coastal and they will make the best of that."

Father had laughed deeply. "Listen to 'em, eh? Experts all."

She herself had not replied, lost halfway down a corridor of thought. She would see him finally, high up and fast, scarf in the wind, taking the corners and cutting the air down the long straights as none had before. She would watch, chained to the ground as he finally crossed the line leaving the competition rolling in his wake.

Then he would smile at the crowd as always. A roll for the men, a bow for the ladies, the greatest air racer in history… "Zephyr St. Charles…" It had been a thought but foolishly she had made it words.

"Zephyr St. Charles!" Della had giggled. "Look at her! That's who she's dreaming of!" She shared a conspiratorial glance with Catherine and looked to their father for approval. He hid his obvious amusement and wagged his finger.

"Don't tease your sister you two."

"But Dad, she *loves* him. She has glossies all over her room! Every race she looks at the news sheets and reads and reads till the words fade away!"

The two of them had collapsed in giggles until their mother, with her usual reluctant sigh, put down her spatulas and pitched in.

"Girls, stop it. Your sister is older. Things are… different for her. She…" She stopped awkwardly. Father had cleared his throat and buried his head in the news sheets.

She'd had enough. Hot and blushing she had fled to her room, the giggles and recriminations fading as she had climbed the stairs.

That blush flourished again as she came back to herself and found her hands on her belly, smoothing the silk of her thin dress against the breeze. The bag lay at her feet. Another blast from the steamer's claxon brought her fully back, and she focussed on the key side once more. The crowds were dispersing, to bars, to hotels, to love, to their business. She picked up the bag and began to walk.

"Alice!" He approached from her right, from the direction of the main road and the academy.

"Alice wait."

She stopped and turned, already knowing what she would see. Andrew was walking... no, marching smartly over the grass. As he drew near she could see the creases in his trousers drawing a shade line down each leg of his uniform. Two red lines marked their sides and matched the red epaulettes on his shoulders. He blocked her path and saluted – the short respectful salute of a cadet. She shaded her eyes once more and said what she thought was expected.

"Hello, Andrew. You look smart."

"Thank, you Alice. You look... pretty. That dress is nice. You look like... summer."

He studied her just a moment too long, then turned to the town.

"Did you see the steamer? It's the second one today."

"The second?" She hadn't known.

"Why yes. They put on an extra one because of the crowds. Apparently there are hundreds on the other side waiting. The Major said there had been some trouble, you know – over there. People wouldn't queue, wouldn't wait properly. Troops were needed."

He said this last importantly.

She shook her head slowly. "But the race is days away. Why do they come now?"

"They want the atmosphere. They want to see the

racers. Anton told me that most are already here, in the grand hotels. They parade with their women and drink on the quay."

She looked away. She hadn't known that either. Maybe she would ask if she could walk on the harbour tonight. Maybe she would catch a glimpse of them, of him.

Andrew pulled her from her thoughts again.

"Would you walk with me, Alice, out along the cliff? I have something to ask you?"

She wanted to say no, but could find no proper reason to. Their childhood friendship had developed, changed, as had Andrew. She assigned this to his age as well as the two years at the military academy. All that had once seemed good now seemed awkward – and in a way threatening. She nodded meekly and he guided her gently with his arm.

"Alice, you know I will go soon. To the war. I will graduate soon – sharpshooter first class. I am, well, I have a talent they say."

Her heart sank a little. Here it came, as it was always going to. She stopped and took a deep breath of briny air, shifting her feet.

"And I would ask you... could I choose before I leave? Choose you?"

There it was, the request, the tradition of years, perhaps centuries, a young warrior choosing his bride before the journey to war. She raised her eyes to his, not wanting to, but drawn by his stare, handsome and fresh. Hopeful but somehow blank, arrogant, daring a refusal. Maybe once, in her younger days she had, like many girls before her, dreamed of this time. But now she felt only dread, outrage at something so predestined, so… assumed.

"Andrew… I…"

"I have spoken to your father. He knows I am to ask you. You must say yes, Alice."

He spoke almost as an automaton. Quick phrases, well-rehearsed. Her cheeks reddened and she pulled from his hand, turning out towards the sea where the sun lowered itself, reddening also.

"You dare, Andrew. You dare invoke that… ritual without leave from me."

Now some hurt crept into his voice.

"Alice, we were young together. This has been planned for years. It is expected. It is my right." At this he took a step forward and held out his hand. She glanced over her shoulder stepping closer to the cliff edge.

"The world has changed, Andrew. The law allows me a choice. That tradition is a relic from the early days of the war."

"But it stands!" Now there was outrage in his voice. "I travel to war, sharp shooter first class. Best graduate for 15 years. I… I might give my life for this land and the land allows me to reserve a wife and to…" He dropped his eyes and tailed off. She spun on him.

"And to? And to what? Oh yes, you stop right there. I will not bond with you now or after your service. When I bond it will be my choice. When and with whom."

She turned back to the darkening sea, flustered, her hands sticky with sweat on the hide strap of her bag. She wrung it angrily. There was silence at her back, and when she turned again he was frozen, staring at her, hand still held out as before. Only his eyes had changed. She might have expected disappointment or outrage, but instead saw for a few moments a coldness, an absence of expression more unsettling than any anger. He stared through her out to the horizon for some breaths, and then, as if summoned back to himself, relaxed. His voice was weak when he spoke, all the fire suddenly gone.

"I see, as you wish. Then I have one more thing to ask."

"Yes?" she was wary now, and still somewhat angry herself.

"The air race, will you accompany me? I can get us close to the circuit. I... I would be honoured."

She lowered her eyes, uncertain. He had changed the subject abruptly, as if something hidden had been decided.

"I can't believe you spoke to my father before me... all these years and I don't know you at all. What on earth did father say?"

Andrew stared out to sea, some of the tension back.

"He said that... that you would decide, and he wished me luck, I thought that..." he paused. "Never mind. The air race... will you go?"

"Luck?! He said nothing to me, and that in itself is monstrous."

In a weaker voice "The race?"

"I will think and let you know. I will think, Andrew."

With that she turned and walked purposefully towards the valley track that led to the town and home. She believed she could actually feel his gaze and the emotions that it sent after her. She felt it leave her too, and turn once more to the sea – and yet another pair of eyes watched her home.

★★★★★

That evening she avoided Father and gained Mother's permission for a walk to the town. There were the usual warnings and alarms, but it was given with a glad heart, as if the woman knew what had transpired on the heath.

The music reached her ears as the first lanterns came on. The conversations and smells reached her shortly after. Main Street to the harbour was awash with activity and noise. The white metal filigree chairs that stood outside the drink houses and restaurants had been augmented by rough wooden benches to accommodate the demand. Eager faces leaned across tables and spoke quickly in unfamiliar accents, the men gesticulating and drinking, and the women, some in coats and fox fur despite the warmth of the evening, laughed to each other at jokes or small conspiracies.

As she approached the Rousillion fountain, a group of whores swept into the street. They were gaudy, loud and lavish, but Alice stopped and stared. How plain she felt in her straight dress and linen shawl alongside their colour and confidence. One of them, a blonde with ringlets, caught her eye.

"Lookin' for trade yourself, dear? There's plenty of competition tonight." Her companions redoubled their laughter. "Mind you, there's some'll take the likes of you before us, just you watch yourself, little miss."

She blew an exaggerated kiss and her earrings flashed, then they swept on through the crowd towards the dock. Alice caught her breath and their perfume hung on her for a short time, its glamour making some promises she felt might never be kept.

She bought some hot flatbread from a man with a brazier and idled towards the harbour. One particularly loud group at a drink house opposite caught her attention. There were about ten people around a table, their faces lit orange by a lantern there, and more standing on the periphery. One man would talk and they would laugh, then he would talk again, animated and smooth.

She dropped her bread to the cobbles and her hands hung loosely, incapable of movement. Zephyr St. Charles in the flesh, air racer and adventurer. He held the small crowd in the palm of his hand, his voice all she had ever imagined and his face even fairer. A dark curl swung over his eye as he whipped his gaze to a slight girl on his left. As Alice watched he took a large drink from his glass and wiped his moustache on the sleeve of his long leather coat.

"…Then I took Gonzales on the inside before the last turn and that was that, last year's final." He slapped a palm on the table and looked across at a tall pale man opposite. "A hard season, eh M'sieu?"

The man nodded slowly and took a drink also. Alice recognised the other from the newssheets – Sir Martin Albury, another gifted racer and a veteran of many years. He was older than St. Charles but, though a former champion, his star had never shone as brightly. She remembered reading of the grand final three years ago, her first season of real obsession. Albury and St. Charles had taken an early lead ahead of the pack and had held it for forty five laps, overtaking each other several times until, the admittedly biased reporter had written, St.Charles had pulled back slightly on the last turn, drawing gasps from the crowd. He had risen briefly into the others wake and suddenly, using the turbulent air had dropped and rolled, his speed increasing to draw a three length lead before the line. The arena had risen and cheered as one. Never had such a risk been taken or such bravery shown in a final. It was St. Charles' fifteenth successive win. Fawning still further, the reporter had then written of Albury's eager landing and his breathless run to beat the crowd surge and congratulate the champion. Try as she might, Alice could not believe the older man had been that pleased to have lost in such a way. Her father – she remembered – had nodded sagely and agreed.

Now her breaths came quick and short, and at the last moment she realised that she had been slowly inching forward, entranced, and now stood agape on the edge of the group. Ten or so amused faces turned to her as the conversation tapered. The slight girl at St. Charles shoulder snorted.

"What's this here, everybody? Look we have a hanger-on! Would you like to choose us some wine?"

Alice reddened but wouldn't catch the girl's eye, aware once again of her lack of sophistication, and her awkward youth. She couldn't pull away from his gaze and all else faded and blurred. He leaned forward, shadowed in the lanterns glow and spoke softly.

"How are you, miss? Would you indeed like to join us?"

"I… no, sir… I would like to… wish you… luck. For the race."

The girl spoke sharply. "He doesn't need luck, child, especially yours."

"Hush, Melody." St. Charles tilted his head while holding Alice's gaze.

"You must excuse my rude friend miss, besides, she is ideally placed to recognise a hanger-on." This to the amusement of all around. "What's your name?"

"Alice. It's Alice."

"I see, and tell me, Alice, will you be at the race?"

"Oh yes, sir."

He leaned closer still. "And are you a betting lady? Will you wager?"

"I… no, no, I just… well my father he…" Her embarrassment grew in the presence of the great man as the words fell out like dice clattering across a table. "He will wager a little…"

"I see." The airman turned slowly to his fellow racer. Albury leaned back with his arms crossed, faintly amused. "Well, Alice, tell your father to lay two crowns on Sir Martin to win!" She was confused and looked around the table.

"But sir, surely you intend to – "

"Shhh." He held a finger to his lips. "And then tell him to lay ten more on me!"

The table erupted in raucous laughter as St. Charles slapped his hand down hard again. Alice looked about, aware she was smiling like an idiot but scared to join in. Suddenly, surprising herself she thrust a hand deep into the pocket of her dress. She felt the charm there with its thin chain, sharp and cold. Her fist closed and she pulled it out.

"I want you to have this, sir!" The laughter slowly stopped and everyone leaned forward. St Charles raised an eyebrow and regarded the small star in her palm.

"And what's this?"

"It's for luck, sir – a charm. It saved my father's life at sea when the boom collapsed, and now he walks with a limp instead of having drowned. He said it only works for a person once but I… I…" She dried up, suddenly feeling foolish and becoming aware of the girl scowling down at her. But Zephyr St. Charles left his chair and knelt on one knee in front of her.

"And it is your true wish that I have this?"

"Oh yes. Yes it is."

He leaned closer still and spoke quietly. "Then, Alice, I shall take it with thanks and wear it with pride, and it will serve me better than any of these sycophants you see here." He held his finger to his lips again. "But don't tell them. They amuse me."

He gave conspiratorial wink and leaned back. "Now, Alice, you must let me get on. I have more tall tales to tell, and I'll bet Albury has some of his own to tire us with."

This last was met with laughter as he turned away, and Alice became aware that she had been forgotten. A final sneer from the woman St. Charles had called Melody confirmed this. No matter. Alice backed away as if in a dream. For a few moments her awe clouded the sounds and the lights, then they slowly returned and she made for home. Whatever darkness had been cast on the day by her earlier meeting with Andrew was now gone, replaced by a memory of a meeting that would remain far longer…

…and from the gloom of an alleyway, from the most recent of a number of secret surveillance points he had chosen since Alice had left her house, Andrew watched. As his fists repeatedly opened and closed, he shivered though the evening still had some warmth.

*****

The road out of town was dusted by a fresh wind from the sea that pushed occasional clouds across a bright moon. Travellers were rare at this hour, and Alice felt a small unease as she became aware of the figure leaning against the stone wall of a small bridge. She relaxed however as it pushed itself upright and began to close the distance between them. Her father's loping gait was unmistakeable despite the darkness.

"Alice."

"Father, I had permission to go, and I am not late."

He pulled up in front of her and sighed with discomfort, rubbing his stricken leg. "I know, child, I'm not here berate you. I've just come to walk my eldest daughter home, and to keep her safe from the wolves that prowl." He smiled broadly. It was an old joke between them.

"I…" She smiled too and relaxed. "Then I shall accept your protection my father."

He turned and began to walk for home. Alice fell in alongside and measured her pace with his, aware of his pain.

"You know, Alice, not all the wolves in this world wear fur."

"What do you mean?"

"Did the boy talk with you?"

She regarded the cobbles for a few moments, embarrassed and then remembering her resentment. "Andrew. Yes. He said he had spoken with you. I was… oh father, I was angry… I am angry. Why didn't you tell me he had been to see you?"

"Because you have to make your own decisions, child, I told him as much. He had a right to approach me. It is tradition."

She bridled at this. "And is it tradition still for him to claim me? To demand? To believe that I would submit just because he was going to war?"

Her father stopped and waved her to silence.

"The brat did that, did he? Well I'm truly sorry, Alice, my girl. I stayed silent because I trusted you to make the decision you did. But you had to make it for yourself, you are… you are a woman now." He snorted. "Or so your mother tells me."

He laid a strong hand on her shoulder. "Daughter, there is something else. There's another reason that you had to see him for what he is."

The moon came from behind a cloud and lit the old man's face, his age lines in relief and careworn shadows beneath his eyes. She stayed silent.

"It is not to be bandied about in the sewing room or playground, girl… Do I have your word on that?"

She nodded, rapt now.

"Do you remember when Andrew first joined the academy?"

"I do, father. He went to the mainland first with his parents and then straight to the army. We didn't see him until his first leave, and then just for a day. I remember we talked about it. He had never shown… never…"

"Never had an interest in the military at all. It's true. He had no choice. There was… a problem with Andrew, my girl, an incident on the mainland. It brought shame on the family, who are, I believe, decent folk. The authorities gave them a choice – or really no choice at all. It was believed that the academy would, well, restore his virtue." He shook his head. "But I always doubted that. All that mattered to me was that your childhood friendship would find, well, a natural end."

Alice raised her hand to her shoulder and squeezed his wrist.

"But I don't understand, father. What could he…" But she did, on some level understand fully, and wondered if somehow she too had a reason for shame. She remembered the boy's eyes on the cliff top, and a sudden coldness spread through her.

The old man pulled her into his arms, and whispered. "There will be no more explanation from me tonight, my love. Andrew will be gone to the war very soon, and we must wish him well. We must hope that they are right and that he becomes a man to be proud of. I doubt he will return to this small island. Once their fighting is over they all seem to need a bigger canvas to paint their lives upon than we can provide here." He paused. "Maybe it would be wise to avoid him until he leaves."

She pulled her head back from his warm chest.

"But he confronted me on the cliff path, surely if you thought there was danger… I was alone and…"

"No, daughter of mine, you were not alone." He patted his wasted leg and forced a smile. "It was a hard walk but I saw you, my girl, and you were safe. I was… waiting, giving you distance and chance to decide… but I was there."

She nodded silently and slowly. Her father's weariness and pain creased his face, and she gave her support as the late summer moon lit their way home.

★★★★★

Some nights later, the same moon threw its light through the gap in her curtains as she slept, and beneath the sheets her legs twitched as she walked through her dreams. Andrew was there, a face in a crowd, his eyes always with that same cold look. She sought to hide as he scanned the faces around him, seeking her out. She would duck behind some passer-by who would immediately move on, leaving her exposed. She was scared and didn't know why, a sense of unacknowledged dread and outrage that was subdued and almost forgotten in the light of day, now became sharp and important. She felt she could read those eyes, as empty as they seemed to be. There was an intention there, a thing to be done and as she sought it out, the dream pushed another idea before her. Crowds moving, noise and hubbub, men rising on the morning breeze, arms outstretched and buffeted by the wind. St. Charles in full flight, his scarf whipping the leather jerkin on his back, alive on the air. With a start she realised this was in fact a waking thought that had embedded itself into her dream. This awareness knotted her stomach with anticipation as she shook fully awake and her excitement pushed the last vestige of her dream to some hidden place, and turned it to smoke.

It was the day of the air race.

Some three hours later, amongst a chaotic throng of people, her mother shepherded them along the road towards the cliff top path. Father followed more slowly with two of his old shipmates, stopping to look and evaluate at each roadside betting stall he passed and trading mock insults or disparaging comments with the ledgermen there. Now and again they would pass one of the town's policemen standing bemusedly at the edge of the crowd, their sense of importance blunted by the overload this special week was having on their routine. 'Move along,' they would say, or rather pointlessly, 'Keep order'.

As the road became a track, and the track crested the cliffs, she saw the markers for the first time. Huge green pennants hung on white poles two hundred feet high. Twenty of them, in pairs, marking out the mile long oval course. They shook and snapped in the wind.

She could see the official tent around the base of the nearest pair of poles, its own green flags marked it as the instrument of the racing federation. Other, less official tents formed an untidy avenue to the viewing area. Merchants, food stalls and musicians, ledgermen, tricksters and jugglers, they all vied for the attention of the excited crowd as it wound past on its way to the race way.

Alice knew that there was a competitor's arena behind the official tent, for countless times she had studied the sheet plans of race meetings, and she knew that it would be thronged ten deep already. She felt, however, no desire push and shove with the masses, straining for a glimpse of the flyers. She had had her unexpected moment in the sun with St. Charles and her heart still quickened at the memory, so she excused herself from the family group and, to her mother's annoyance, strolled to the periphery of the crowd. She noticed here that the majority of people were off-islanders, business people or city sophisticates, drawn to her homeland by the glamour of the racers. Slender women, wearing pencil skirts, and with soft fur around their necks, giggled and pointed. They stood in groups, or as one half of a couple, arms linked and holding tight with the thrill of it all. Their beau's would nod wisely to each other, commenting on race strategy or snorting contempt at someone's predictions for the outcome.

Alice, lost in thought and memory, and with mounting excitement at the prospect of the race, wandered further away towards the cliffs. She approached a rocky outcrop some twenty yards from the cliffs and watched a lark settle in the grass next to it. Dimly she registered a voice, amplified by loudhailer, announce the contestants, and she

knew it was time to return. Soon the men would rise on
the wind. Soon the men would fly. Before Alice could turn
however, the lark took fright, startled as someone stepped
from behind the outcrop.

Andrew. Andrew with his cold eyes. Andrew with a
long shoulder bag and uniform clean and pressed.

She caught her breath and took a step backwards.

"Andrew I…"

"You whore." He walked quickly forward, dropping
the bag onto the grass.

"What?" A sharp fear touched her.

"I saw you with him. Saw you whoring yourself with
gifts and words. You never even saw fit to acknowledge my
invitation and yet you flaunt yourself at him."

"With who? What do you mean?" But she knew who
he meant, and now she knew he was entirely mad."

She walked backwards unsteadily, and glanced over her
shoulder to the crowds, more distant than she had
thought, and looked for her father, more distant still.
When she looked back, Andrew was advancing quickly, his
cheeks red. Now she felt anger and stopped.

"How dare you, Andrew? How did you know I'd
come over here?" He stopped too, a smile spreading, more
threatening even than his eyes.

"I didn't, my love. It's a happy coincidence. I was here
for another… appointment."

He ran the last few paces and grabbed her arm,
squeezing. He pulled his face close.

"You are mine, not his. You always were."

He pulled her off her feet and dragged her towards the

rock. She screamed, but he beat her to silence with his free hand, stopping only to retrieve his bag.

Time slowed down for Alice then. He punched her in the stomach as she tried to rise and lay on top of her, pinning her legs. She coughed but then pursed her lips as idiot kisses and breath played on her face. Her dress and knickers tore, and then there was more pain. Unfamiliar pain, sharp yet slow. She dug her fingers into the warm grass and screwed both eyes shut, sobs jerking free as the boy's weight moved on her.

…And in the midst of the horror a sound. The sharp crack of a pistol followed by a mighty cheer. The Air Race was underway. Irrationally her eyes opened and some part of her that was separate and detached from this violation strained for a glimpse of the flyers… though they were hidden by the dark rock, and that part returned to the pain…

Andrew let out a long groan and pushed himself away, adjusting his clothes urgently and scrambling over to his bag. "Now you're mine. Now you'll see," he repeated, breathless himself. She lay, wet with tears and some blood, and stared miserably, no coherent thought able to form, just a mute witness to the scene.

The boy positioned himself against the rock, invisible to the crowd and pulled a long rifle from the bag. His movements were rushed but precise. A twist on the sight, a break of the grey barrel and a single bullet in the breech. For a few moments she thought she would die now, but as he braced against the stone and wiped the sweat from his eyes, he turned skyward, and the certainty of what he intended fell suddenly upon her.

The air moved above them as the racers passed by. The outer reaches of the first turn passing over their solitary rock. Two hundred feet high, the men parted the air before them, switching and swerving for position on the second lap. A blur of leather and silk, they would pass over this spot forty eight times more before the finish. Irrationally and for just a moment, Alice felt an excitement as the crowd noise reached her ears, cheer upon cheer. She rolled painfully to her knees and watched the departing racers, a blur of colour as they reached the third turn above the distant pennants. Then the situation took hold and she frantically crawled towards the rock.

"No, Andrew, no!"

He was forward against the stone, his long barrel tracking the prey. Another few seconds and they would be overhead once again. She remembered his boast – sharpshooter first class – but surely not at this speed, this distance. Ignoring the ache between her legs she struggled to her feet. He spoke without turning his head.

"Too late, whore."

A crack cut the air, a sharp report – the second of the day – and she stopped. The lead racer fell away from the pack, flight position gone and flailing like an injured game bird. Alice froze and silence fell upon the invisible crowd.

"You… you… No!"

It was St. Charles, his colours unmistakable. Injured but not dead, for every few seconds he would regain a morsel of control and slow his fall, then tumble again, speed increasing. She saw that his trajectory would bring him close. Just over her head. To the cliff. Some thirty feet from the ground he stiffened and slowed, not enough to soften the impact but enough to stop progress towards the edge. Alice spun on her heels as he passed low overhead and crunched into the grass some ten feet from the cliff, rolling once and then lying still.

She staggered towards him, oblivious to Andrew, oblivious to the silence that had fallen upon the day.

"Sir? Sir?" She fell to her knees and laid hands on his twisted body. He was breathing deeply and fast. There was dirt on his pale skin and blood on his leather. So much blood. He was trying to speak, eyes wide and confused, but his words splintered in his throat. Alice cradled his head now, her tears falling on his face, and noticed her charm, given in love and in hope, around his neck.

St. Charles briefly focussed. "Why… why, girl. What is this?"

"Be still, sir. You are undone by a madman. It is none of my doing…" She leaned her hands onto his stomach wound now, applying pressure. "And… And yet it is. Please live, sir, they will be here soon." She turned in panic to the arena. Sure enough the crowd had gathered itself and distant figures moved quickly towards them. He strained to lift his head and regarded himself.

"My girl… I am lost. My life slips from me and I don't know why…" He narrowed his eyes. "Why you are the girl from the town. You are…"

"I know, sir. I never meant this. I just wanted to fly… to fly like you and race and, and now Andrew has – "

Andrew.

There was pain before the sound. An unbelievable

132

pressure, sudden and massive moved through her back, and her body arched, coughing as it fell onto that of the flyer. Their eyes met and struggled for focus, both uncomprehending but both certain of death.

"And now, sir… I can't tell you for I too am undone. My father will… oh my dear father. He will…" She could not form a thought, could not express coherent outrage or grief. St. Charles eased himself up and looked at her back.

"Oh my lord, girl. You are worse than I." He looked to where Andrew crouched some yards away, fumbling as he reloaded.

"You monster. What have you done? What is all this to you?"

He received no reply, and bent his head close to Alice's ear.

"My girl, he means to finish us, we must… you must hold tight. If we are to die today it will be on the wind."

Alice breathed heavily through her pain, failing to understand for a moment. Then she felt it, coming through his hands as he gripped her. A wild electricity that moved to her spine and up into her head. Their bodies lightened and shifted slowly, scuffing the grass of the cliff top, moving towards the edge. She could hardly see or breathe now as the wound inside bled her life away, yet she marvelled at what she felt as they moved. He was sharing with her, giving some of his gift through contact.

"Do you still want to fly, little one?"

"Oh, sir." It was little more than a whisper. "It's all I have ever really wanted."

He pulled her closer still, pressing her face into his

leather jacket, and they lifted a few inches further. She could not believe what she felt, even through the mortal pain. This then was what the flyers felt, every time. Many had tried to describe it, and now she could see why their words had fallen short. A stretching, a cramping, an energy. A freedom.

St. Charles lifted them upright on the air and over the cliff edge. She was dimly aware of the surf and rocks some 200 feet below as they turned slowly to face the approaching crowd and their young assassin. Men threw themselves at Andrew, falling on him as they wrenched his rifle away. Alice saw them stop and stare, frozen to the spot as they regarded the couple hovering and swaying. A woman screamed and pushed through the throng. Her mother. Her father would be far behind, slow and unsteady. She lifted her gaze and looked into the flyers eyes.

"Sir, I… thank you. We can go back now. We can be treated. Maybe…"

He shook his head slowly.

"You child, not I. I choose the air and the sea."

The energy moved in them again, as with one colossal effort he propelled them back towards the edge. She could feel him weakening by the second as with one last pirouette he swung her to safety and let her fall onto the short grass. As the crowd rushed to her she reached for him, gasping.

St. Charles gave one wave and a small, sad smile as he raised his hands to the sky. Then the life left his eyes and he slipped from her view, his body becoming loose as the accelerating wind played with his limbs. He fell to the cold sea below. Alice felt gentle hands upon her but ignored them along with the awful pain. They rolled her onto her back and a circle of faces framed the afternoon blue and towering cumulus. The clouds called to her. They spoke of a life on the wind, free of pain and care. They spoke of mysteries hidden within the recesses of their white and grey canyons.

She closed her eyes and answered.

THE BLUE

July 16th 1969

You won't find Pellow's Field on any map now. Its
runways lie buried and mostly forgotten beneath the urban
sprawl of St. Margaret – itself a place of lost ambition and
failed enterprise among more prosperous and lucky towns.
The airfield closed in the '40s, after the carnage of France
and Holland. Its few instructors and recreational flyers
either moved on or were shot to pieces fighting for their
idea of freedom amongst distant clouds.

The blue still wheels above it though, and every sharp
Florida morning seems to hold the promise of those early
days, and an invitation to share the joy of that cold, high
air. Does the sky above Pellow's Field look down and
wonder where its children have gone? Nah, of course it
doesn't, it has new wonders to witness. Those few of us
left however, sure as hell look up and think back to those
glory days. At least I do.

You won't find me on any map either. I too have been
buried, not by Tarmac and sand, but by time and
indifference. I push the dinner plate and the brown mush
that sits on it away across the table and scan the room.
There are a few residents left, lounging in the overstuffed
chairs, reading magazines or mumbling conspiratorially to
each other, or occasionally to themselves. Most left for

their rooms after the initial spectacle of the launch, either believing that the excitement was over for now, or disappointed that the mighty needle had not exploded on the pad. They wouldn't admit it I'm sure, but some folks are like that.

One of the carers takes my plate.

"Y'all finished up, Mr Tomlin?"

"Sure am, son. Tastes like shit as always."

He ignores me. What does he care? He nods towards the TV, where some commentator holds a large microphone in the face of a NASA official.

"Y'see the launch? Jeez, we're on the way to the moon. Who'd have believed it?"

I nod and raise my eyes to his.

"Yep son, I saw it." I say.

He leans closer now.

"Say, you alright there, sir? You look kind of shook up. I seen you in the chair all day. Were you waiting for the TV? Making sure you had a good viewing slot? Maybe you need some air."

"Maybe I do, son. Maybe I need some high cold air."

"Say what?"

He's easily confused this one, so I wave him away. I had been waiting for the launch alright, been waiting these 41 years…

July 16th 1928.

There were two ways a man could fly at Pellow's Field in those days. Either you had money and you owned a plane, or you were good with your hands and you fixed them up. I was the latter, having moved into aero-engineering from the auto trade some years back. I had worked hard for my licence, and been fascinated with aviation since childhood. The Great War had seen the technology accelerate, and now we were all fired up with Lindbergh's great feat of the previous summer. The place was busier than ever, and on the up.

The Alexander Eaglerock biplane was waiting for me that morning, that's how I figure it now. Royal blue and grey, she sat on the turf, expectant, gleaming. I pulled up in the lot and smelled the air. Florida sunshine, avgas and oil. I was where I wanted to be.

"My brother of the blue!"

Judd Harris waved from the hangar door, a cheroot dangling from his lips, swinging his feet as he sat on the oil drums. Jeez, you'd never get away with that now. Health and safety has eaten us up, chewed the adventure and charm out of it all and spit it out.

"Yo, Judd. It's a fine day. Thanks for getting her out."

I indicated the Eaglerock. She was brand new, owned by John Chevitt of Chevitt tyres, St. Margaret. Chevitt was self-made, and one of the new breed of blue collar aviators who were slowly stealing the skies from the gentleman flyers of old. The skies were becoming democratic. I'd taken delivery for him the week before, checked her over and sorted the paperwork. He'd paid with grateful thanks, and my flight today was a kind of gratuity. I felt a little patronised, but hell, I was going flying. Part of me thought that he figured that if she was going to fall apart on her first proper flight, it would be Ray Tomlin that bit the earth and not him. But what the hey…

I fuelled her up and did a walk around, running the numbers in my head. Curtiss OX5 90 horsepower engine, crushing speed 135mph, range just shy of 400 miles. A beauty, fit and eager for this wonderful morning.

I swung by the office for my flying jacket, goggles and cap, and picked up old Judd on the way out.

I indicated the prop.

"Do what ya should, Judd."

He gave a casual salute as I climbed aboard and moved around to the front. Fuel on and primed, controls free, tap the compass rose. The needle did a curious 360 in its oil and settled. This stopped me for a minute, but then I tapped it again and it seemed to float free. I never gave it another thought, until later...

I strapped in, then...

"Contact!"

He swung good and hard and stepped back. She fired first time, and the roar of the Curtiss filled the world. Judd yanked the blocks and I eased her out towards runway 090, one of the two turf strips that made up Pellow's Field. It would be a straight climb out, and then I planned to turn north and follow the Atlantic coast up towards the cape. As I ruddered around into the sun, I noticed a line of cloud over the coast, some three miles distant; this was contrary to what had been forecast. Maybe it would change my plans, maybe it wouldn't. We were more wary of cloud back in the day. There are old pilots, they said, and there are bold pilots. But there are no old, bold pilots.

Screw it. One last control check, a wave to the tower and a glance at the drooping orange sock and let's go. I opened the throttle and the Eaglerock leapt forward, smooth and determined.

'Mr Chevitt,' I thought, 'this is one fine bird you've gone and bought.'

A short, bouncing roll later, a pull on the column and we kissed the grass goodbye for a while, greeting the sky with a small whoop. Despite the plugs, the noise was huge. Few folk realise that most of what you hear from a propeller aircraft is the noise of the blades breaking the sound barrier, and not the engine. From the cockpit, the experience is different to that of an observer on the ground, to whom the buzz of an approaching aircraft integrates into the day slowly, either an intrusion or a call to adventure, depending on your point of view.

We levelled out at 700 feet and scanned the coast. That cloud was solid alright, seeming to hug the beach as often happens when it hits the warmer air of the land. I reckoned the base at 1000 feet, and it didn't look that thick, maybe 300 feet. No problem. Not yet. I broke off some chewing gum and made some lazy turns, looking for anyone else who may be up here this fine day. There was no one to be seen. I reckoned to get above the cloud before I got to it, then I could turn north as planned and be ready to race it inland if it began to move or form.

I think I was at about 1200 feet and just beginning to see over the top to where the sunlight turned it into a flat silver grey sea, when I noticed the compass rose again.

"Son of a bitch…"

The needle was spinning, refusing to settle, although I was flying due east and true. I tapped it again to no effect.

Then the world went grey and cold. Where the hell that cloud came from so fast I will never know. Likewise, how it expanded or formed around the Eaglerock and me, when seconds before it had been some minutes away. The compass was still acting out its craziness, and for a minute I was totally disorientated. We all know the drill, in cloud trust your instruments. I ignored the compass and clocked the artificial horizon, which said I was still straight and level. Ok, what to do. I had an instinct to hold my heading and get down below the grey as quickly as possible. However, that would put me over the sea, which was fine in theory, but would be just another step on the road to the 'incident pit' if anything else whacky happened.

I knew I had to climb out of this. However fast the cloud bank had spread, it couldn't have thickened much in that short a time. Clouds didn't do that. No, they didn't do that. I pulled back on the stick and opened her up a little more. The airspeed stayed constant. The Eaglerock's engine wasn't troubled at all by this small demand and I held a constant rate of climb for a minute.

At 1500 feet there was still no sign of the sun, or even a lightening of the grey fog whipping past. Ok, this would make a good whiskey story later, but for now there was another decision to be made. I maintained my rate of climb and counted out what should have been a 90 degree left turn. By my estimation this would line me up with the coast, and not take me out over the brine while I worked this shit through.

Now, at that time I had about 1000 flight hours under my belt and two peachy forced landings to brag about, so

I can't say I was scared at all, just a little confused and irritated by this turn of events. The gum had lost its taste already, and I spit it out to my left and looked up.

Sure enough, the grey was lighter, then it was tinged with azure, then a deeper blue, and then we broke free, and once again the sunlight wrapped around us, gold and silver, cool and clear. The sun was behind me and to the right, which meant I was heading north where I'd intended. I looked inland, over the edge of the chasm of cloud, at the patchwork of fields and the shine of lake and river. Way up ahead the arc of the Cape curved around northwest, just about covered by the rolling grey carpet that still spread below me. I allowed myself a smile...

... And I held that smile, crooked and frozen for the next minute or so as I tried to process what I was really seeing.

I think I can say that I knew the country below me pretty well. Eight hundred of my hours had been out of Pellow's, both under instruction and beyond. Almost every test flight, every recreational hour had been spent looping and wheeling above these fields. What I saw below me now, over the edge of the cloud, just shouldn't have been there.

Buildings just too big and too square. Hangars? Warehouses? Too big for sure. Roads where none should have been. The altimeter read 2000 feet, which sounds real high to you ground bound folk, but it ain't. From that height I could recognise my car in a full lot, almost wave at the guy trying to steal it...

There was a town. Melbourne? No, far too big. It

sprawled. There was just too much down there. Highway One ran parallel to me, but there was something wrong there as well. The road was too wide, and the wrong colour; it was also almost entirely devoid of traffic. I could see the beach, running and curving towards the cape, where it disappeared into the grey layer of cloud. I banked the Eaglerock to get a better look. The beach made up for the highway. There were thousands there, standing, just standing. Not in the waves, not at barbecues, just standing. This was all wrong, wrong in a way I couldn't understand.

This place, wherever I'd flown myself to, was waiting for something. I got a sense that the world was holding its breath.

That's when the engine began to misbehave. Least ways, that was my first thought. There was a deep throb now under the regular buzz of the Curtiss. It swelled as I listened close. I have weather-ear for engine trouble, and this sounded big. I scanned the instruments, and apart from the compass that still seemed intent on screwing itself from its mounting nut, all seemed fine. The undertone grew to a roar with an accompanying shake. That's when I began to get scared. I peered through the windshield, looking for tell-tale black smoke from the cowling, and that's when the world changed…

The featureless spread of grey cloud had spread inland and covered the Cape entirely, and from the flat plain of vapour she rose. From a distance of just under a mile, she appeared as a black and white column, heading skywards, vertical and true on a cascade of bright fire. She was an aircraft of some kind, but bigger than any I knew existed, and she needed no wings to get her where she was going. The roar that she made – and the source of my imagined engine trouble – came with a vibration now that physically shook the Eaglerock, seeking out loose bolts and wayward linkages.

The thing must have been rising fast, but because of her size, she looked to be climbing painfully slow, struggling to overcome the gravity that must be clawing her back. The Eaglerock and I seemed to be heading directly for her, or rather the smoke stack which trailed the fire she rode on. I can't tell you what I felt, for I felt nothing at all. I had no room to assimilate or process reactions. I simply observed. Here alone in the noisy wild blue, I beheld a thing that defied understanding. Afterwards, sure, I would try and connect this with the compass and the strange landscape below, and sure, I would wonder at the men who had caused this magnificent thing to be.

The machine – for that is what she surely was – rose higher, accelerating. The sound of her passing began to fade as she climbed into the darker sky above. Whether she was a weapon of war, or a means of transport, she was going where she was going by design, and that was somewhere very high, and I was sure, very far away.

Then something sparkled off to the right, in my peripheral vision. I tore my eyes away from the great ship in front of me and the world changed again. Whatever I had been chosen to witness that day, I wasn't quite alone…

The vision, the experience, the memory as it would come to be, lasted for about a minute, then something passed and she was gone. I felt a physical release from something I had never even realised had a hold on me. I was over clear fields, the peculiar buildings gone, and the landscape back to what should have been. More notably, there was no cloud layer. It hadn't drifted or broken up. It just wasn't.

The compass read 360 degrees – true north.

There was just the Eaglerock and I, the roar of the Curtiss, and the whip of our slipstream. I started to breathe deeply and quickly, making up for the rapture of the last two minutes. I wiped a glove over my forehead, and it stained with sweat and oil. As I eased the stick to the left and headed back to Pellow's Field, I began to try and reason, to tell myself what I'd seen.

I had to work a way to explain it to myself. Sure as hell I would never tell another soul.

"My brother of the blue, you don't look so good. The old Eaglerock scare ya, huh?"

"No, Judd, guess I'm just coming over with a chill."

"Want me to stick her in the hangar for ya?"

I mimicked his salute of earlier.

"Do what ya should, Judd."

July 16th 1969

I'm alone in the sitting room now, watching the TV with the sound turned off. Once again I drift back to that day above the cape. Of course, as the years sailed by, and history caught up with itself, I began to realise what I'd seen. When the first footage of Hitler's V2s appeared on the newsreels, I died a little inside, thinking that what I'd witnessed was a vision of the end of days. It was only when that conflict ended for the best, and both sides of the new world order began to tinker with their satellite programmes that I felt a little easier. Then I watched, rapt and eager, as we developed Mercury, and then Gemini. I watched the monochrome launches from the Cape and became certain for the first time of exactly what I'd seen.

Then Kennedy had boasted about the moon, and they'd rolled out the first Saturn 5. All of a sudden there she was, that monster, that wonderful giant that I'd somehow shared the sky with that cold clear day in 1928.

Had I physically been there, or had nature just hiccoughed and played some weird trailer to me? Of course I have no way of knowing which launch I'd actually seen. I'd checked the weather detail for each one, and there were no records of a strange, fast moving bank of stratus over Florida for any of them. I've concluded that it was a symptom or cause of the event, and visible only to me. Something inside of me however, knows that it was Armstrong, Aldrin and Collins I'd seen, forty-one years to the day in some possible future, and our first great howdyedoo to a world beyond ours. I want to believe that.

In all the long years that laid themselves out from 1928, through the desperation of the depression and then the war that followed, I think I was able to hold onto something denied to most. Whatever hate and despair the world threw at us, and whatever Hell we made for ourselves, there was hope. At least this one moment of glory waited for us.

So what sustains me now? Now that the glory days are gone, along with the dreams of young flyers and their stick and string machines? Now that the old skills of sky and sea and mountain have made way for digital backups and systems beyond our imagining back then? Now that all I have left is a shared TV and brown mush three times a day?

Well, I saw something else on July 16th 1928, something less easy to explain.

Even though I'd never chosen to, it would have been possible for a man from 1928 to describe to you a Saturn 5 rocket, even if his terms of reference are somewhat skewed. But I can't describe the other.

Not at all.

Let's call it a whisper in the sky, a lattice of light, a craft of some kind or maybe a window to another place. I just know that I shared the vision that day with something 'other', something that had come to see, whether by design or, like me, by accident. If you think that now I've seen the moon launch in its true time, I've caught up with my future, you're dead wrong my friend. There's a lot more, a long time more. The world stretches away from us like a clear sky, it contains death and sorrow, cynicism and hate, but it also contains hope and the promise of wonder – a little piece of the blue.

ALBION'S SHORE

I recall that day on the cliff top, standing bent into a sou'wester as the rising wind thrashed the crowd, and the ocean broke it's chaos on Albion's shore. My cap sought to fly and I wrung it between my hands as we watched.

Two men flank me, entire opposites; my father to my left, thin, frail and well meaning, but reluctant here at the land's margin. He stands duty bound to his son's request, but sees no purpose in our mission, and resents every gust or fleck of rain to shake or stain his business suit. The sea captain is at my right shoulder, barrel-chested and dense as a rock, his beard is plastered back to red cheeks, but his bulk dares the wind to move it.

Two sets of sails on the wide water, bent on a broad reach and tight with the air that feeds them. Two great tall ships cutting neck and neck through the swell; the *Sea Maiden* out of Fairstead Sound and the *Cutlass*, fashioned from the old oaks that crowd the hillsides above Sanland Bay. The last of their line, locked into the endless race for trade rights and fighting still for honour and gold.

I step back from between these men and look to the flock of townspeople gathered with us along the sharp cliff. Forewarned yesterday of the vessels' approach, they have left their businesses and homes to watch this spectacle.

Both ships have cleared the Western Cape now and though they will come no closer to land than this, those without spyglass or bi-lenses can still catch the form and speed of each. Those who have dug out or begged such tools however can see more – the pale majesty of a full, fat sail, or the spider forms of men as they scramble aloft, trimming and tying. They can see the crystal spume as both vessels cleave the ocean before them, and the gleam of brass from the rails as the sun and spray play with the moving light. They may even see the legends themselves; Masters Abraham and Thorn, the respective captains and rivals, both carrying the hopes of their companies and communities, both carrying the weight of prosperity or lean times. Most folk here however hold no wish to be out there. Most will gaze and fawn over what we see today and be content to return to the safety of fire and factory.

Unlike me, son of a ledgerman and raised in a house of numbers and a steady wage, they will never taste the brine, nor wish to…

"Y'see the *Cutlass*, lad?" The captain's voice is deep against the wind. "She's drawn half a length ahead. That's to be expected mind. She's more square sails aloft, and can run faster before a wind such as this."

"The lad won't understand, sir." My father has moved closer and placed a hand on my shoulder, as if to protect, to claim ownership. The captain raises a bushy brow.

"That so, boy?

I look to my father as I reply.

"I understand well enough, sir. It's not just the sail area. The *Cutlass* sweeps more sharply back from her bows, and then drops dead to the keel. She has advantage there too."

Father shakes his head and removes his hand. The captain laughs deep.

"Blow me. He knows his stuff, sir. He'll have a life on the waves I'll bet."

"No!" It's too loud and spoken with protest. The captain and I regard him with surprise. I feel a strange sorrow, and a curious sympathy for this man who has raised me and my siblings with steady toil and income, but who doesn't know, or seek to understand me. He stands embarrassed.

"I mean… David, the boy. He will follow me. He will work the numbers and balance the sheets. This is what our family do."

The captain sighs. "Aye, I dare say he will."

He winks and we fall to silence, turning once more to the sea. Both vessels have now traced half our visible horizon and ploughed on, from Cape Strath on our left to the black needles of the wrecking teeth at the far end of our home cliffs.

"Come boy, your mother will rag me for getting you wet. Your boats will be gone soon."

"Father, you said we could watch them cross. It's once every three years and I can't remember the last time."

I see him stiffen. He is deciding whether to remain bound by his hurried promise, or to renege, and spirit me away from the threat of the captain's words and their challenge to his authority. I feel for him, and I know he loves me. His life is, however, bound by the conventions he learnt so long ago, and now seeks to impose on me. He hides my picture books, he lifts my knot boards to the high shelves, and he steers me from the harbour when we walk the dogs. The ocean is forbidden to me, and this man is the threat made flesh.

"Look, boy!" The captain is pointing. "The *Sea Maiden* has reeled her foresail, she intends to – "

"Jibe!" I beat him to it. "That's her advantage, she can turn through and steal their wind."

"Aye boy, she can. Abraham will play to his strengths and make advantage. They both need more sea room now the wind is rising. Mind, Thorn is no slouch. He has played this game before, and he knows his boat like his own hands."

"It's a dangerous game though." My father has chosen to engage. I know he will make his case for the safe path, for the numbers. "There are those out there today who won't return." This last is spoken directly to me.

"Aye, that's true enough," the old seaman nods, "but those that do will have stories to fill their old age."

"...and that old age will be spent with bent and broken fingers."

"They will see the aurora shine on the broken northern ice."

"They will be blind from squinting."

"They will lay themselves down on the warm sand of the Sayn islands and feel the sun as those dark lovelies kiss the salt from their lips..."

"Sir, really... the boy has ears."

"...and if they're lucky, as was I, they will hear the song of mermaids as they sing to the moon from their perches on the grey reef."

"You, sir, did not see mermaids. Or hear them."

The big man shrugs.

"Maybe not, sir." He throws me a wink. "But I chose a life that allows for the possibility."

That does it for Father. He holds the captain's eye and slides his hand down my sleeve feeling for my hand. I can hear the mermaids.

"Come, David. We're for home now. You have your school work, and the dinner will be warm."

I look to the captain as I am pulled away. He turns to face my father, all beard and brass buttons. He holds out his right hand.

"Sir, I did not mean to offend. Take the boy home and see him warm. Then he'll be warm for life."

It's a curious thing to say.

My father stops, uncertain. Then releases me and takes the man's hand.

"No offence taken, sir, you have your life and we have ours." He forms a thin smile and nods. I take a last look across the waves. Both vessels have cleared the rocks and are passing from view. I am led away from the cliffs, and steered between those who still stand and lean against the blow. Then there's a deep voice at my back.

"Can ye tie a bowline, boy?"

I pull against my father, turn, and speak my last words to him.

"Aye, sir. Up the hatch, round the mast and back down the hatch."

A deep laugh is quickly swallowed by the wind.

★★★★★

And I am swallowed too. The cold waves close over my head and the long fall to the deep begins. Glowing metal falls past me, bubbling its heat away as the shards of broken cannon and hatch seek the ocean floor, far fathoms below. The sharp cries of the wounded are fading, yet I can see their legs kick and flail, moving for wreckage and life ring.

Off to my right, in the wake of the pirate's dark hull, the ocean is on fire.

I made my decision five years after that day on the cliff top, the winter that the 'fluenza finished my father. My older brother Tom took hold of the house built with numbers and I signed on as a hand on the *Mary's Hope*', leaving Albion's shore for good.

The years have been long. They have been hot and they have been cold. I've seen those lights in the northern climes and I've kissed many of those girls. We've hauled grain and coal across many good seas, and enough bad ones. Memories vie for attention now at the last. I discard most with no regrets, and yet hold to just one.

It was born on an airless day off the Grey Reefs one distant August, standing amidst the men lazing on the deck as still as the air. I imagined a musical voice that rose for a few moments and fell silent. I'd moved to the stern rail and turned at a movement from the corner of my eye. I think I remember a smile framed by a slick of dark hair. I seem to remember a flash of aquamarine as the sunlight moved on scales, a tail quickly eaten by the sea, and a sense of what may or may not have been.

I have to conclude now, with the last reasoning that my last breath allows, that I, David Rome, lately Skipper of the *Sea Maiden* out of Fairstead sound have never seen a mermaid...

...but I chose a life, and that life allowed for the possibility.